A NEW WAY TO REMEMBER

ONE

Every small grief that had ever slid into a remote crack of memory emerged to swell a tsunami of sorrow that was pounding against Maya's ribs. Her stomach clenched, her chest convulsed and her mouth stretched wide in a prolonged wail. It was a phantom cry. John was sleeping peacefully beside her and it was essential that his equanimity be maintained. It was a Zimmer frame for her often daunted spirit; moral scaffolding that prevented such nocturnal distress from crashing into daylight. He believed that, together, they had put her past behind them but she was unable to shake off a persistent fear that any echo from that past could harm them. She had not dared to tell him about the phone call that had brought it so dangerously close again.

She turned to him. He was gone. She must have somehow fallen back into a troubled sleep. Panic gripped her for a few painful moments. There was something difficult and demanding to be faced and she was not ready for it yet. She reached out and touched John's crumpled pillow, convinced she could feel his lingering warmth, reminding herself that she had fought so hard, gained so much and come so far. This was no time to falter. She got up, put on her dressing gown and pulled the belt tightly round her waist, as if holding herself together to meet the immediate challenges of the day ahead.

John was sitting at the small table in their bright kitchen reading the paper. Maya stood behind him, put her arms round his neck and rested her cheek on the back of his head breathing in the faintly citrus scent of his aftershave. He reached for one of her hands and kissed her palm and then, as she moved away to make toast and tea, gave her a look for which she could find no precise description. She was still learning this unspoken language of his. She needed words and the hold that they gave her on every kind of experience, but even in mundane situations he used them sparingly and where emotions were concerned he tended to mistrust them.

She was aware that when they met he had been led by her appearance into believing even more strongly than usual that language could be unreliable. She had the fair skin of her English father but was slender and small-boned, with her mother's thick, black hair and dark eyes. The faint, almost bruised, circles under those eyes emphasised an exotic heritage, or worse than that an ambiguity, that unsettled people. Usually, as soon as she spoke their anxieties were allayed. Her vocabulary and intonation were reassuring. John, though he was clearly drawn to her, had been troubled by less easily appeased worries and fears. That they had been appeased was, for her, a miracle.

"I thought that we should leave in about an hour. If we get to Mother's early, I can manage a few odd jobs for her before lunch." He folded the newspaper. "You still seem a bit blurry around the edges. A bit sleepy. You haven't forgotten that this is visiting day?"

Her slight, sideways smile acknowledged his attempt at a humorous tone. They spent every Sunday at his mother's cottage and it could be awkward for him. Sensitive to her

2

mother-in-law's suppressed disapproval, she was finding her hard to like, and John not only loved his mother but, his father having died nineteen years earlier, was very protective of her. Maya, who had major issues and minimal contact with her own divorced parents, felt unreasonably threatened by this. Ashamed of such mean-spiritedness, she always made an extra effort over these outings and took trouble to dress more conservatively than usual for them, discarding her jeans and vivid cotton tops for simple skirts and blouses and pulling back her often unmanageable hair into a neat knot. She saw these visits as the price she had to pay for John.

Getting along with Maya was the price Joyce Carter felt had to be paid for keeping her son close, or as close as any grown-up son can be kept, given that families tend to become fixed, somewhat randomly, at points along a sliding scale of intimacy. John, at twenty-two, had left home to find a flat near his workplace and, initially secure in the memory of his happy childhood and relying on that history of happiness to hold them together, Joyce had fairly soon been shaken by passing references to unshared moments in his new, separate life. His marriage, the biggest worry that he had ever caused her, was a minefield through which she walked so carefully and self-consciously that she only added to any pre-existing tensions. She was sure that he loved Maya but it was not a love grounded in common experience. This wasn't the natural, easy-going kind of relationship that she was used to and had wanted for him.

"So," her neighbours had said, "John's going to disappoint all the local girls. Only to be expected, now he's living in Cambridge, that he'd find one there. What's her name?"

"Maya. Maya Fielding."

"Maya! That's unusual."

"It's Indian. Her mother is Indian."

"Well now!" Their eyes had slid away, but not before she caught the fleeting, shadowy presence in them of media-induced images; veiled women, bearded men, fleeing crowds, armed policemen. In Norfolk, they all felt far from these topical concerns but, even here, reinforcing a traditional wariness around strangers, there was an uneasy awareness that nowhere was truly safe. Not like it used to be.

Nothing was like it used to be. For years, pulling garments from her wardrobe, Joyce had glimpsed in the mirror on its door the pleasantly plump, even pretty, person she had always seen and had until recently continued to see. Now, this familiar, imprinted figure had vanished. Because a new person in her life would not share that familiarity, would view her objectively and possibly unkindly, she had examined herself more closely. Disconcertingly confronted by an elderly woman with untidy, greying hair, she found that getting dressed each morning now took much longer and, on Sundays, more time than she had ever spent on herself before she was ready for the day.

Hadleigh was no picture-postcard village but a straggle of houses along a stretch of the main road that for about three quarters of a mile was designated, with typical East Anglian matter-of-factness, The Street. Four side-roads led off this and the Carters' house stood at the far end of one of these, backing onto fields.

It was no picture-postcard cottage but an un-compromisingly square, flint building with the stark simplicity of a child's drawing; two windows on either side of a dark wooden door and two above on either side of a smaller, circular one. It was fronted by a neat gravel drive, some fiercely shorn lawns and two round flowerbeds in which plants were aligned and spaced with regimental precision. Like some mischievous scribble on this illustration of solid respectability, a surprisingly ramshackle, lean-to conservatory ran along the right side of the house, furnished with two faded, unmatched chairs and a large pine table upon which, among an array of small cacti in terracotta pots, stood a large basket of eggs and a stack of egg boxes. Below it there were several open bags of compost and some sacks of chicken feed.

Maya had first seen all this three months after getting to know John. All that time he had made it clear that he always spent Sunday at home and it was only when, at last, he had asked her to come with him to meet his mother, that she knew his feelings for her had overridden his doubts about her. That day, as they had pulled up on the drive, Joyce had opened the front door and stood waiting on the stone step, neatly dressed in a blue silk dress, her grey hair as close cut as her lawns, every strand as carefully arranged as her plants. John had leapt out of the car and gone over to hug her and Maya, on full alert, had caught his whispered comment.

"It's the first time I've seen *that* door opened in a long while. Don't worry, Mum. Relax."

Three Sundays later, when Joyce came out through a side door in the conservatory to greet them, things were a little less strained. The day that she finally emerged already draped in the large white apron she wore when cooking, Maya could even believe in the eventual possibility of some degree of understanding between them.

Nine months after their first encounter and six months after she and John had married, this was still only a possibility. But if conversation was never entirely easy, lunch was now less formal. The best china had been returned to the corner cabinet in the dining room, with a few smaller pieces in the same positions of honour in its glazed upper section that they had always occupied. They ate off the daily china, some very old willow pattern plates supplemented by modern additions. Not all the serving dishes matched but the food was always delicious and Joyce determined to see every bit of it eaten.

"More chicken? Take more vegetables. Try the carrots. They are from the garden."

Today, Maya, as usual the main focus of this insistent hospitality, could for a split second smell curry. Five years old, in India for the first time ever, sluggish with an excess of food and the humid heat, she was sitting at a large, polished table surrounded by a crowd of noisy, gesticulating strangers and her Indian grandmother was ladling food onto her plate. "Eat. Eat. Try this. You will enjoy it. I had it made especially for you. It's very mild."

"What do you think, Maya?" John's voice broke into her thoughts.

India faded; the air was cool, chilly even; she was an adult, obediently helping herself to carrots. "Sorry, I was daydreaming. What do I think about what?"

"I was asking Mother to come to *us* for a change. She could spend the weekend. She hasn't ever stayed at our house and we could take her out for a meal."

"I can make a meal." Maya knew that she sounded sharp, aggressive even. She hadn't answered the main question but leapt instantly to a defensive position.

"Of course you can but it would be a treat for both of you." John was unruffled.

"We'll leave it for a while, John." Joyce smiled at him. "I find it a treat just having you here. It gives me a chance to do some serious cooking. I tend to get sloppy eating on my own. I'll come sometime later in the year."

"We'll be pleased to have you." Maya knew this was an inadequate response and that her tone was not exactly warm and welcoming, but it was the best she could manage.

When they got back to Cambridge late that evening, there was a message on the answering machine. "Maya, you haven't called." The voice was light and breathy. "Have you decided where and when I can see you? As I told you when I rang the other day, I'll be in London for such a short time. I have to be in Bombay in eight days. Darling, you can't still be furious with me. Be sensible. That's all over. You're almost twenty three years old. You're a married woman. I have to meet this husband of yours. I am your mother. The whole thing has become impossible, ridiculous. I need to hear from you at once."

"Your mother's in England? She called you? " John turned to Maya with a slight frown. "When?"

"Two days ago." She caught his hand. "I know I should have told you but I... well... I... I'm trying to... I suppose I am just hoping she'll go away."

"Maya, whatever is wrong between you, you can't act as if your mother doesn't exist. She's right. It is ridiculous that I haven't met her. She must feel hurt. Especially since she probably knows that I have already met your father even if only briefly and belatedly. We need to deal with this. We'll ask her to come here." He saw her horrified expression. "It's an easy train ride from London. She can come just for the day."

"No! I don't want her here. I don't want her anywhere near here."

John stared at her, his eyebrows raised. Her eyes dropped and she bit her lip. His face softened and he reached out, pulled her to him and kissed the top of her head. "It's OK. It's OK. Leave it to me. I'll fix everything. As she's in London, I'll find out which hotel she is staying at and where exactly it is. We'll go up on Saturday and see her there."

TWO

The lobby of the hotel was not as luxurious or welcoming as its ornate, pillared facade led Maya to expect. The monochrome severity of beige walls and flooring was barely softened by two tall palm trees in metal containers, set beside a seating arrangement of angular, leather chairs around a glass-topped table. Such austerity was certainly in tune with her taut, controlled reluctance and John's cool neutrality but this seemed an unlikely setting for her mother.

Then, just as they were moving towards the reception desk, a lift door opened and there she was. Her dark hair was cut in a short, asymmetrical style and she was wearing a red trouser suit, its slim-fitting western design somehow given an indefinably oriental flavour by a vivid, multicoloured scarf, elegantly draped round her shoulders, its ends falling down her back.

"Darling!" She rushed forward, her arms outstretched, but as Maya took an instinctive step away from her, they fell to her side and she stood rigid for a moment. John moved quickly, holding out his hand.

"It's good to see you, Mrs Fielding."

"Please! Call me Soshan. Mrs Fielding has become a bit irrelevant and you can hardly call me Mother. I'm a stranger." She flashed him a wry look. "This business of what to call your in-laws is *so* difficult. I never knew what to do about that myself at first. Luckily, to begin with, Peter's mother – I believe that you have already met my ex-husband, Peter – well, his mother was not at all thrilled about our marriage and I rarely saw her. When I did, we hardly said anything to each other. Later, as she began to miss her son, she learned to tolerate me and came to see us more often. By then Maya had been born. That solved the riddle. We called her Granny."

"It's nice to know that I was useful, not just a mouth to feed and a nappy to change. That gives parenting a whole new dimension, babies as a solution to social dilemmas." Maya caught sight of John's suddenly grim face and felt a momentary panic. She had to be more careful, try not to take things up where she and her mother had last left off, a battle over but the war still on. She leant forward with a forced smile, made as if to touch her mother's arm but pulled sharply back.

"You're rushing into things as usual." She tried to speak lightly. "Perhaps we should keep the family history for later."

"Sorry, quite ridiculous, but I'm actually a little nervous. That always makes me rattle on. It would be best not to subject John to such a history at all but some things about us are bound to come up." Soshan surveyed the lobby. "This place looks a bit stark. The restaurants are much more cheerful. I thought you might prefer to eat in the coffee shop rather than have a formal lunch in the dining room, with waiters hovering at our elbow throughout. We can fetch a drink from the bar first, if you'd like one. That way we'll be able to find a quiet table straight away and allow ourselves time for a good, long talk."

Maya's blunt announcement that she was about to get married had been a surprise; that the wedding was to take place five days after her letter containing the announcement was posted had been a shock. Sending a letter had clearly been a deliberate tactic because the whole thing had, in fact, been over by the time the news arrived.

Cambridge
17/12/13

Mother,

Just to let you know that I'm getting married on the 22nd. My husband-to-be is called John Carter. He comes from Norfolk and works in Cambridge, where we shall be living. We are planning a very brief, simple ceremony at eleven in the morning at the Registry Office and Dad and John's mother will be the only people there. We are having lunch with them afterwards. John and I are then catching an afternoon train to London, where we will be spending Christmas. It seems impractical for you to come so far to have such a short time with us. Don't get angry with Dad as I said that I wanted to be the one to tell you about this. John's mother was the only person that we told earlier. I had already met her often and he wanted her to get used to the idea of a modest affair with no guests. She wasn't too pleased but she has taken it well. She would support John in anything he does. They are very close....

A chronic ache, so longstanding as to have become normality, had flared up in a moment of acute, breath-stopping pain. Soshan was more hurt by this casual cruelty than by anything Maya had ever done since refusing, at the age of fourteen, to come back with her to Bombay. Though not exactly forgiving of his part in the stormy, sometimes vociferously argumentative, sometimes icily silent, disagreements that had finally ended in divorce, she had insisted on staying permanently in England with her father. She still had at least two more years in school and this had clearly been the only possible arrangement during term time, but she had adamantly rejected any suggestion, then or later, that she should spend even holidays in India. Peter's widowed mother had very readily stepped in to help him out with her granddaughter's care. Conscious of her mother-in-law's sense of vindication for years of covert hostility, Soshan had bitterly regretted having thoughtlessly delegated such duties to her when Maya was a baby and had felt a visceral reluctance to do so permanently, but this had been outweighed by a desperate need to flee her own unhappiness and a country where she had never had a sense of truly belonging and where there was no longer even the pretence of any real support for her.

Peter had always been fairly conscientious about sending reports of their daughter's progress in the early years after their separation but, gradually, he phoned or wrote less often. They had not spoken to each other for over two years and, driven to call him over Maya's latest exploit, she had been shaken to hear his deep voice again. "It's been a shock to me too, Soshan." He had sounded tired. "She hardly confides in me and since she went off and got herself a job and somewhere to live in Cambridge, I've rarely seen her. I knew nothing about John until just before their rather spartan wedding and I only actually met him on the day prior to that. He insisted on our having a private talk. He wasn't comfortable with the way they were doing things but he wanted to make things easy for Maya. I have no idea what she has told him about us. I imagine it was all quite dramatic. Anyway, I am very taken with him. He's eleven years older than Maya but I see that as a good thing. Even at twenty-two she still seems a bit immature. It's not so much her age as her general attitude. She does so many things simply with a view to annoying us that it's hard to know what she really wants. I sometimes wonder if she knows. I think John will be a steadying influence. He's very serious, has a reasonable job and there is a rural background that features a large farm which, I gather, belonged to his grandfather, passed to a childless uncle and might one day be his. All credit to him, John's not taking that for granted and is getting on with a career of his own. Some sort of agricultural research in one of the Cambridge laboratories. He clearly loves Maya. It looks as if she loves him. She will be alright. I think we can stop worrying about her."

"So he loves her." Soshan's voice dripped scorn. "You once said that you loved me, Peter, and you know what came of that. There's a song about love being just a four letter word. You have to admit that, between us, a four letter word is exactly what we reduced it to. In any case, it's very open to interpretation. We all make it mean what we want it to mean. It's no magic incantation, no cast-iron guarantee. I realise that I haven't been the kind of mother Maya wanted but I have been the only kind I can be and, despite what she thinks, I do constantly worry about her. It's been so long since I last saw her. I want to come over as soon as possible and inspect this new husband."

"Stay away." Peter's voice had been harsh. "If you want this to work, I suggest that we both leave Maya to settle down. She wants to start a totally new life. We owe her a chance, some freedom; not least from us."

The coffee shop was indeed an improvement on the lobby. Tall windows, opening onto a town garden, let in pale sunlight which was reflected in huge mirrors on the opposite wall and this, together with the cane chairs and bright tablecloths, gave it an outdoor feel. It looked a more likely place for friendly conversation, but after they sat down at a quiet corner table there was an uncomfortable silence and they all took refuge in the menus. Soshan, using hers as a screen, sneaked a surreptitious glance at John. He was not exactly handsome but with his sturdy build, springy, dark hair and striking blue eyes, definitely attractive. She adjusted her scarf and checked her hair in the wall mirror behind him. Maya, looking up, caught her flicking her fringe and frowned.

"What exactly are you doing in England, Mother?"

"I told you when I phoned. I've started working for an English friend, someone your father and I knew in India. She has opened a shop selling Indian handicrafts and I've been sourcing things for her at my end. She wanted me to see how things are run here. Get a better idea of what exactly she needs. She's introducing me to one or two other people who are also interested in what I might do for them."

"Does that mean regular trips?" Maya was frowning again.

"No, that won't be realistic for some time. It's still, from my side, a very small operation." She hesitated and then continued, her voice slightly tremulous, "This is a business trip but I felt that it would give me a chance... that it was time... to get to know John and hear a bit about what you've been doing since I last had any news of you. I hear so little about you. I have a phone number but I'm not even sure where exactly in Cambridge you live."

"Not actually in Cambridge. We rent a small, semi-detached house in a nearby village called Neston. John drives us into work and we travel back together in the evening."

"Your father told me about John's work but he didn't appear to know what exactly you are doing." Soshan's face was carefully blank. "You don't seem to have had that much to do with him lately."

"As always, he's usually engrossed in his own work," Maya said sharply. "We keep in touch in a general way. That's always been good enough for both of you."

John snapped his menu shut. "Tell me what drinks you'd both like and I'll go to the bar and get them. They're on me, Soshan, and I'll treat you to lunch as it's our first meal together and something of an occasion. Meanwhile, Maya, you could tell your mother about your job. It's not exactly classified information."

His tone was even but firm. Maya's shoulders lost their rigidity and giving him a placatory smile, she turned to her mother and spoke more gently. "Dad said that he told you about the intensive secretarial course I did while I was still staying with him. He obviously hasn't told you that I have a job at the lab where John works." Her eyes met Soshan's with a shade of defiance. "I needed to get something with a degree of permanence. I'd been flitting from this to that too long."

Soshan said nothing, her fingers playing with the ends of her scarf and her face still unreadable. Maya took a leaflet from her bag and set it down on the table. "That's the place! It's an important research centre but I'm not involved with that side of it. That's John's field. I'm just one of the office staff. Actually, I never saw myself doing anything like this but I'm surprised at how much I enjoy it. I like the regularity and the predictability. You would no doubt prefer me to be doing something more upmarket. Something a bit more impressive to tell your friends about."

The set of her chin, the slight curl of her lip – an expression, seen so often during her teenage years, that could not be called a smirk but hovered somewhere between provocation and satisfaction – awoke a remembered irritation in Soshan. She felt the urge to give her the sharp slap that she had so often resisted in the past.

"My friends are rather more enlightened than you ...." Catching sight of John coming up behind her with a tray of drinks, she stopped short and turned to him with some relief.

Over lunch, by tacit agreement, the conversation skimmed the surface of their lives as if their only interest was in timetables, distances, room dimensions, the colour of curtains, the vegetation and climate of Norfolk. Then, as they were finishing their coffee, Soshan spread her hands wide and taking a deep breath, looked steadily at her daughter.

"I need to know about more important matters than your journeys to work and your decor choices. I want you to tell me everything about yourself; how you really are; when I can come to visit you."

Maya retrieved her handbag and stood up so abruptly that she almost overturned her chair.

"There's no time for all that. We can't stay any longer. We have to get back to the station. There's a train at three. If we go now, we can walk."

"Don't be ridiculous. Of course you can stay. You wouldn't spend the weekend here but you don't have to leave until the evening. We'll go for a stroll in a park somewhere, have tea and take a taxi to the station."

"No. Sorry. We have to go." Maya was already stumbling away from the table, moving blindly through the cafe and towards the door of the hotel, her face shuttered and stony.

Soshan turned to John, pale and dismayed. She had suddenly lost her aura of glamour and he bent towards her and said gently, "I'm so sorry. What can I say? I knew, of course, that Maya had problems with you and her father but clearly things are very much worse than I thought. I don't know what's got into her." He gave her a level look. "This isn't really a business trip is it? It's bad that you felt the need to approach us so cautiously, to have a cover story, and hard that it's all gone so wrong."

Soshan rubbed her eyes wearily. "It's my own fault. I was a terrible mother." She drew in a breath like a half sob. "I only thought about myself and now I'm left with only myself to think about."

John took her hand. "I hate to leave you like this but I must find Maya. It's probably best to let her go. I really am sorry. Here, I've written down my e-mail address. I'll keep in touch. That will be easier now that we know each other. Don't give up. I'll do what I can. We'll work things out." He resisted an urge to kiss her cheek and walked briskly away but as he reached the door, turned to give a small wave. She stood where he had left her; erect and smart in her scarlet suit, forlorn but brave. He could see a very real resemblance to Maya and his heart lurched.

After her swift walkout, Maya had stopped outside the hotel and was leaning against the wall, waiting for him. "John, I...."

"Don't say anything. Right now, I'm both furious and upset. I don't want to talk to you. I feel like dragging you back inside and making you apologise to your mother but that might make things worse. I can't trust you. Since you are in such a hurry to get back, we will make an effort to catch that mythical three o'clock train of yours."

He strode off, giving her no chance to answer and she followed, almost running in an effort to keep up with him. Once at the station, they used the surrounding crowd as a buffer, uttering only the minimum of necessary words and keeping a clear distance between them.

As soon as they reached home, had opened their door and entered the hall, Maya turned to John, flung herself at him and wound her arms round his neck. "I'm sorry. I'm sorry. Don't give up on me. Don't be angry. I'm sorry."

He disentangled her clinging arms and held her away from him. His voice was cold and forbidding. "I am really worried about your mother. It was quite appalling to have to leave her like that and you gave me little choice. I had to follow you. You have behaved disgracefully. You know that. Your mother is naturally distressed and *she* has every right to be angry. But anger seems to be what has landed you all in this mess. We'll leave it for the moment. No need for a drama. I think we've had enough of that for now. Of course I won't give up on you. But you obviously haven't told me everything I need to know. You must stop hiding things from me."

Maya managed a watery smile. "I don't think I do hide as much as I suppose." She closed her eyes for a moment before opening them and blinking away tears. "If I try, it's because I'm so afraid that you'll regret ever meeting me. I've told you about the divorce and how wretched, how lonely I was as a child but it's so much more complicated than that. My parents are... I was... well it was a total disaster." She clung on to him again. "I want to forget it all. I don't want you to be caught up in it. I want us to be quite free of it."

"Maya, no matter what went on between you, they are still your parents. We have to be realistic about that."

"Don't look so fierce." She stroked his cheek. "I can't talk about it until I've cooled down and had time to think but I promise that I'll be sensible. No more dramas! I'll do something sensible right now. I'll make us a drink."

She tried another faint and apologetic smile and turned to go into the kitchen, glancing down at the phone on the hall table as she passed it. "Oh no! There's another message. It must be from Mother." She stood as if frozen and John came over and pressed the button.

This time, unusually, for she rarely called, it was Joyce. "John. I hope you had a good time with Maya's mother. I always think of London as a challenge, though, and if you'd rather not come tomorrow after a tiring day out, there's nothing ready for lunch that won't keep. It's just that your uncle has stirred himself and asked us all for tea at the farm. It's been a rare event of late. Robert has his notions. He's only asked us once since you started coming here with Maya. She has never really seen the place properly. I think she should. I also think that your grandmother should have a chance to spend some time with her. I dare say that you might feel the same and would like to go. Let me know by tonight if you are coming."

John picked up the phone to call back and Maya went into the kitchen and closed the door behind her. She did not really think that he would reveal much of what had taken place in London but he couldn't ignore it and she was fairly sure that he would warn his mother against asking too many questions. Whatever he would say about today, however he would say it, she did not want to hear it.

THREE

The next day, bright with sunshine, cooled by a soft breeze, was one of those perfect early summer days that are, in Norfolk, overarched by an endless sky, a pure, vast emptiness, extending behind and around the clouds that drift within it. It was a day that defied unhappiness. It felt like an undeserved blessing.

Joyce almost certainly puzzled and upset by the little that she did know about their London outing spoke of it so carefully that she had clearly been coached by John, as Maya had supposed she would be. Over lunch, as it had yesterday with Soshan, the conversation stayed very matter-of-fact. Maya described their journey, the hotel, the work that her mother had come to do, stressing that for her this was a business trip and a very short one.

"Luckily," Joyce said peaceably, "the world is so much smaller now. India isn't as far away as it used to be. Well, obviously it is, but it isn't difficult to travel to, or from, anymore and that makes it seem nearer. If your mother is working with people here, she is likely to come again soon."

"I hope so." John looked meaningfully at Maya. "Next time, maybe there will be a chance for you two to get together."

They set out for the farm at about three. It took fifteen minutes to walk there through the village. It was possible – on wet days preferable – to reach it by leaving the road, going through an elaborately arched gateway and following a wide drive towards an imposing house set in formal gardens. Hadleigh Hall had once been served by what was then the Home Farm and was still connected to it by a pathway that led off to the left between high hedges. Those elegant days were long gone. The landed family who had once owned most of the village had moved away, having sold their house, the farm and most of the surrounding cottages. The Hall was now owned by a company that used it as a conference centre and the farm, though still known by its old name, had been bought by Joyce's father and inherited by her brother, Robert. The weather being fine and dry, they did not use the drive but went a little further on beyond it and turned down a sandy track that, after a short distance, opened up onto a wide lawn and a very substantial farmhouse.

Though it had not been designed and built to a plan but had evolved over the years, time and vigorous climbers had softened all the lines and joins of its disparate additions and extensions, mellowing brick and stone and even flint, until now it was impossible to imagine it as other than it was – a solid if rambling, square-centred, many-windowed, plant-shaded and inviting house fronted by a high porch and flanked by a range of equally solid barns and outbuildings.

Indoors, the rooms were spacious, dim and cool. To the right of a wood-panelled hall there was a large sitting-room with an enormous fireplace, now filled with an elaborate arrangement of dried leaves and flowers, and as they went in, a thin, angular man with a weathered face got up from a high-backed chair beside this and, making no attempt to greet them beyond a brief nod, bent over a very old lady dozing in a smaller chair on the opposite side.

"Mother. Wake up. Here they are. Here's Joyce with John.... and Maya."

For a second, Maya found herself caught in a surprisingly vivid blue gaze; a momentary spotlight; John's eyes, but looking out at her from soft wrinkled pouches; a sharp focusing of some undiminished force within the frail, bent body of his grandmother. Then it was gone as Joyce brushed past her brother and moved between them.

"All right, Mother? That's a lovely day. You and Robert are missing all the sunshine. Maybe you could come outside into the garden for a while before tea. Don't want to sleep all afternoon or you won't sleep at night."

"Hardly all afternoon, Joyce," Robert's voice had an edge. "Just an after lunch nap. It's good for her and she gets outside often enough. She still manages to potter round the garden most days. And she sleeps like a log. In fact she was in the garden this morning, so she's best to stay indoors now. Why don't you take Maya for a walk? It was bad weather the first time she came here. She hasn't seen anything of the farm yet. We won't have tea for a while and I want to have a talk with John."

Joyce's mouth tightened. Maya, who had never seen her anything but placid and self-controlled, was surprised by the hostile look that she flashed at her brother.

"Everything planned then, Robert?" Her voice was harsh. "Well, it was never any use going against your plans. We'll get out of your way. Come on, Maya." She strode out of the room and Maya, looking back rather doubtfully at John, followed her.

"Do you need anything?" Robert turned to his mother. "I'm just taking John into the office. We'll have tea in about an hour."

"You go on. Don't worry about me. Give me a kiss, though, before you go, John. Robert is always fretting over things and hurrying us along these days. I haven't had a chance to say a proper hello to you. And I'd like to see more of that wife of yours."

"You'll have time with them both over tea." Robert was already halfway to the door.

John, giving his grandmother a quick kiss on the cheek, hurried after him across the hall and into the large room that had been the farm office for as long as he could remember. Breathing in its mingled scent of tobacco, dogs and leather, he was for a moment, a small boy again, knee-high to his grandfather, Nathan Cole, dapper in a tweed jacket and spotless jodhpurs and, as always, gaiters so highly polished that, even in imagination, he closed his eyes against the shine.

"Well, John." He came back to the present, hearing, not Nathan's deep, country drawl but the lighter, more anodyne voice of his uncle. "How did things go yesterday? What is your mother-in-law like?"

"Ah! That's what this tea party is about. You aren't given to idle curiosity, Uncle, so what's worrying you?" John sighed. "That's a silly question. I realise that you think that I've married a foreigner." He leant towards his uncle, his face flushed. "Maya was *born* here, her father is English and she has always lived in England. She is English. But, of course, she *looks* different. Mother has had a struggle with that but I think she's getting over it." He shook his head and sighed again. "What no-one realises is that Maya has a struggle with it too. It's hard for her when people can't accept her for what she is rather than how she looks. And, by the way, her mother is as smart as paint, more with it than most of the women you come across here. She belongs to a community you may never have heard of, the Parsis. They are mostly business people and her family are wealthy and highly educated. She isn't some illiterate villager."

Robert sat down heavily at his desk and made a business of shuffling some papers piled on it. He too was flushed. Neither he nor his nephew had ever been men to show their feelings and this outburst had clearly thrown him. But, after a brief pause, he motioned John to sit down.

"I have seen the doc recently. I'm only seventy-two but there is a bit of a question about the state of my heart. Father went without warning at about this age. Mother always looked so tiny and frail beside him but I think she'll outlast me too in the end." He cleared his throat and again flipped through his papers. "It's always been understood that you'd take over the farm one day, but I wanted to tell you that I've now made the whole thing totally watertight and legal." He sat up straighter and looked directly at John. "Nothing to be gained by beating about the bush. Maya's mother, whatever she's like, isn't English and she doesn't live here. Though in practical terms that doesn't alter anything, it does concern me. I'd like to think that the farm will always stay in our family. What about your children? They'll have foreign connections, a foreign grandmother."

"Good God, Uncle, you've seen a doctor for the first time in ages and that's led to this? It may be years before you're written off. And even when I take over, it's going to be a very long time before we have to look any further ahead than that. Will farms like this even survive? What will technology do to change things? You've already changed them in ways that would have shocked your father. We can't behave as if a feudal system were still in place. Even if we can count on the survival of the farm, any children that I might have could be uninterested in it. We can't run their lives before they are even born. One thing I am sure of; Maya will make certain that her children feel one hundred percent English. That's something she's always wanted for herself."

There was a long, uncomfortable silence. Both men unnerved not only by the level of self-exposure that they had been drawn into, but by what they had revealed to themselves.

The back door of the house was at the end of a tiled passage that led out of the hall, past a wide staircase, the dining room, the kitchen and two side passages. It opened into a walled vegetable garden, laid out in neat, formal rows of raised beds but given a rather more rakish air by bright red and yellow tulips pushing up, as and how they could, through a mat of dying daffodil leaves that straggled on either side of a central pathway. In one corner there was a small, rather dilapidated run built up against the wall, housing a few hens.

"This was once my mother's territory." Joyce stood looking round somewhat ruefully. "There used to be several runs, all along that wall, and large numbers of poultry. Now that she can't manage anymore, there are only these few left, to provide enough eggs for the house. For years, she always dealt with and sold all the eggs we produced. Otherwise she had no say in how the farm was run. Or even the house, come to that. My father was a very forceful character. I used to help her here. This was one place where we did things together. A place where the men left us to it, to do what they saw as women's work."

Maya glanced uncertainly at her, not knowing how to respond to this surprisingly frank reminiscence. She was struck by the thought that this was the first time they had ever really been alone together or discussed anything beyond day to day matters.

"But Mother was much tougher and more independent than I realised. Look at her now. Ninety-three and still carrying on. I was often angry with her as a girl. She used to only ever think about what Father and Robert wanted. Especially Robert. For her the sun shone out of him. I always felt totally unimportant." Joyce's lip turned down and the ghost of that old resentment flared briefly in her eyes and died. "Well, I got over that. I found a quite different sort of man to either my father or my brother. He made me feel very important."

Maya, suspicious of this seemingly innocent, but possibly deliberate, reference to mothers and anger, simply could not think of anything to say.

"Come on. I'll show you where I got engaged." Joyce walked briskly across to an arched gate in the far wall and unlatched it. Coming up beside her, Maya found herself looking out, not over the farmland she had expected to see but over a wide meadow. A meandering stream, visible as an occasional glitter among tall reeds, flowed under a low bridge in the distance before disappearing in a wooded area of slender trees and bushes.

"Has John told you much about his father? He was only fourteen when Fred died and it was very hard for him. He rarely talks about it."

"He hasn't said anything about how he felt. He has told me that his father was born in London and later was an accountant in Norwich. I know that you met him when he came to the Hall for a conference and that soon after that he gave up accountancy and started to work on the farm. John said that your father gave you the cottage. He explained that usually workers get a tied house that goes with the job, but yours was an outright gift."

"Yes. My father liked Fred well enough but, because he wasn't ambitious and was content to be little more than a farm-worker, didn't actually think much of him. It made him feel successful and powerful to give us that house. Well, to give it to me, actually. He had a strong sense of family and property. Robert's the same. Very old fashioned that is now."

Confronted by this acid-tongued version of her mother-in-law, Maya felt increasingly disorientated and at a loss. For nearly a year, they had been circling warily round each other, always under John's eye. They had perhaps begun to settle into something a little more comfortable recently but nothing that would have indicated this level of openness. Was it anything that John had told her yesterday or was it something about returning to her old home or her mild confrontation with her brother that had fired up Joyce?

"We were walking out there in that meadow when Fred asked me to marry him." Joyce's voice had softened. "The sun was shining like today. I said yes without hesitation. We were so young. Both total innocents really. Finding each other was pure luck. It was all very simple; no story

28

book romance; but we were very happy. We did have one terrible loss but then we had John. Then I lost Fred too. It sometimes seems to have happened long ago and sometimes only yesterday."

Though Joyce, pensive and abstracted, appeared to be caught up in a private world, reliving a very personal story, Maya could not entirely rid herself of the feeling that her mother-in-law was challenging her in some way that she could not quite understand.

"We won't chance walking out there." Joyce was her normal, practical self again. "Even after a few dry days, it's probably very soggy. We'll go out through that gate over on the right. I'll show you the farmyard and then take you into the kitchen and introduce you to Mrs Hemsby."

"Who is Mrs Hemsby?"

"She's the wife of one of the farm workers. She's been coming in for ten years or so to clean the house and since Mother has become frailer she's taken over the cooking too. Mother's always had help. A succession of village women. Father was an important employer for local people though they saw him as an outsider and didn't really totally trust him for a long time. He accepted the fact that these women gossiped about us. Still, they added interest to our lives as children. I especially remember one, when I was about ten, called Mrs Beard. She had this terrible habit of belching and saying, "That has eased my poor body." Robert and I used to giggle about her all the time. Just her name was enough to set us off. That's why I remember her. It was something Robert and I shared – and we never shared very much. My father couldn't stand her. With hard work and, I suspect, quite a bit of dealing, he had really prospered but he wasn't educated.

Yet he was a fastidious man. It wasn't that he tried to be genteel. He genuinely disliked anything rough or coarse. So! Goodbye Mrs Beard. Mrs Hemsby is a much later arrival but it looks as though she will be here forever. Sometimes I think that Robert and Mother will be here forever. The Coles are part of the place now." Joyce moved off impatiently. "Come on, let's go. I don't know why I'm rambling on like this. It must be showing you round for the first time."

Maya's sense that she was being challenged, that there was a message in these uncharacteristic outpourings, grew stronger but another quick, searching look at Joyce revealed nothing out of the ordinary.

She had never been on a farm before and she could not know how far from the frequently muddy, shambled mess of a typical yard, Robert's was. And if this neat, paved square surrounded by low, tiled buildings was like an illustration from a child's picture book, the kitchen could have belonged in a magazine, though slightly more comfortable and slightly less smart than such carefully photographed arrangements, with two shabby chairs and a scuffed pine table that had crept in to bring it down to earth.

Mrs Hemsby turned out to be a small, wiry woman of about sixty, with sharp eyes that gave Maya an unashamed once-over. "Tea's ready, Joyce. I've helped your mother to the table and called Robert."

Tea seemed an inadequate word for the spread laid out on a crisp white cloth on the dining-room table; cold meats arranged on a large platter, a deep bowl of salad, bread and butter, scones, biscuits, assorted small cakes and a three-tiered jam sponge on a cake-stand.

"Come and sit by me John." His grandmother patted the seat beside her as the men came in. "Maya can sit on my other side. Such a pretty wife you've found yourself. Don't worry about her. Don't let Robert bother you. Everything will be fine."

"Mother!" Robert gave her a warning look. "Have some tea. Don't witter on."

She glinted at him and turned to Maya. "I wasn't ever pretty. When Nathan, John's grandfather, brought me here after marrying me in Lincoln – that's where my father farmed – local people were very stand-offish. I was small and as brown as a berry from working outdoors. I knew full well that there was a rumour he had found himself a gypsy, but in the end they came round, eager enough to be friends with Iva Cole at Home Farm. Even now, I don't lack visitors. But I haven't forgotten how ready they were to look down on me in the beginning. How lonely and homesick I sometimes felt. But I stuck it out. No use giving in."

Robert and Joyce exchanged looks and, apparently in accord for once over the danger of letting their mother continue in this pointed vein, rushed into speech simultaneously, gave way to each other and made sure that they kept the conversation within safe limits for the rest of the meal. Iva, whose age had hardly diminished her appetite, said little more and ate heartily. Once they had finished eating, she was clearly drowsy and, helped back to her fireside chair, instantly fell asleep, only half waking sometime later to say a rather muddled goodbye.

After walking back with Joyce, John and Maya eventually set off on the return journey to Cambridge much later than usual. It was getting chilly. Wispy patches of mist were rising above some of the fields that they passed and floating out over the road. This seemed to Maya to reflect her state of mind. She had set out that morning with her ideas clear and her attitudes fixed but this unusual day had made life more complicated and her head a little hazy.

"OK, Maya?" John was never a talkative driver.

"Fine. A bit tired that's all."

She was far from fine. Joyce's disclosures, following immediately upon yesterday's fiasco, had cast a strong light on what had, until now, been unquestioned realities and she was feverishly mulling over some hard facts. That stupid and unforgiveable confrontation had resulted from an obsession with her own resentments and heartache. It was slowly dawning on her that it was this obsession rather than the past itself that might well damage both her and John.

Many relationships grow organically like plants, sharing the same soil, developing slowly and naturally but theirs had shallower roots and, though both exciting and affectionate, had always felt potentially fragile. For the first time she considered the thought that this fragility was not due to any possible falling away of John's love for her but to her shameful readiness to see their marriage in a more utilitarian light, to look on it as an escape from all her dissatisfactions. She had taken for granted that John was there to rescue her, make total happiness finally possible for her. But why had she assumed that he would do all the giving? Today, she had caught a glimpse of sadness and secrets in his background; his rather unconventional grandparents; the death of his father; the unexplained loss that his parents had suffered and for which he had been an apparent compensation. Her vision of his untroubled, country boyhood now seemed to be one of the simplistic stories that she tended to tell herself when trying to get to grips with life. It was painful to admit that, though she was not solely to blame for the unfriendliness between them, this had fuelled the undoubted envy that had bedevilled her interactions with Joyce. Had her mother-in-law been trying to set the record straight?

She half turned to look at John and was reassured by his placid expression and the sight of his strong hold on the wheel but almost immediately terrified by the extent of her need for such reassurance. She could look back at a long list of failures – hers and her parents. But relying on him to compensate for all that she felt she had missed out on was perhaps the worst and most dangerous failure of all. The other people in her life had their own needs. They would not always act with her in mind. A stab of mingled fear and love made her reach out and rest her hand on John's knee.

"Careful!" He nodded warningly at the road ahead.

"Sorry." She withdrew her hand and sat primly upright. Nothing was ever simple. Even love and affection had to be shown appropriately and as required.

FOUR

Seven o'clock on Monday morning. Somewhere high above Europe, her legs in compression stockings, her feet encased in embroidered slippers, her skin oiled to prevent dryness and her ears shielded by rubber earplugs against the drone of the aircraft and the buzz of fellow passengers, Soshan found that there was nothing that could protect her from her own thoughts. She had an open novel on her knee, one that she had long wanted to read, but having got up at four and been through the twenty-first century horrors of an early morning airport, she was still too physically drained to concentrate on a printed page. There was nothing to distract her from her own story.

In the nine years since her divorce, there had been many times when remorse, self-hatred even, had taken and shaken her. She had been twenty-one when she met Peter. He was then three months into a one year posting in India, having been sent out by his bank to work on an internal re-organisation and gain some overseas experience. His blonde good looks, deep voice and forceful self-confidence had fascinated her but she saw now that she had fallen in love not only with him but with the idea of change and adventure. She had seen herself as romantic and daring to marry outside her community and against the advice of her parents but this mild rebellion had given an added dimension to their breakup. That failure had meant more than losing a husband. It had meant losing face. Hardest of all – and somehow, despite all the difficulties between them, something she had never foreseen – it had also meant losing a daughter.

Within her close-knit group of cousins, there had been those who, even as quite young girls, had always longed for children, for whom marriage and husbands were a means to that end. She had never experienced such maternal urges. She had indeed half believed that it might be best for her and Peter not to have children; children who would be exposed to the pull of conflicting cultures. But Maya had been born, such a pretty, beguiling little creature that she had immediately adored her and was glad not to have deprived herself of this pleasure. It was not unalloyed. In the early days, when living in England had been a novelty, it had been fun to play at housewife but with the added work involved in caring for a baby things became rather more irksome and, if she were truthful, frightening. She had missed the flow of voluble, affectionate parents, aunts, cousins around her. They would all have shared the responsibility for this new life, a responsibility that would have weighed lightly on them, their carefree acceptance of it so encouraging in comparison with the seriousness of all the professionals who offered her solemn guidance and then left her to it.

She struggled on for the first months. Then, finding in Peter's mother a doting grandmother, disapproval oozing out of every pore yet still only too keen to take care of Maya, she had gone for two short breaks in India. She had suggested taking the baby with her but had been too easily persuaded by her mother-in-law that this would be disruptive of the child's routine. She had not felt especially guilty about these temporary retreats. She and her two sisters had been largely looked after by ayahs and given a sense that, while she loved them, their mother had other concerns and interests that had to be respected. As long as a woman managed her household and servants well enough to ensure that her children were healthy and thriving, it had been considered natural that she should also enjoy an independent and active social life. In England, of course, with no helpful ayahs and caught up in the constant care of their children, most parents allowed them to become the centre around which they organised their lives. Soshan soon understood that in choosing Peter she had tacitly agreed to another way of life and had finally buckled down to this more demanding style of motherhood and domesticity. He had offered little help, making the decisions that shaped their lives but leaving the realities of carrying them out to her. His energies were focussed on his career progression within the financial world in which he operated.

It became increasingly and humiliatingly clear to her that his Indian adventure had been out of character, undertaken solely to further that career. She was crushed by the chilling realisation that their marriage had been for him more of a misadventure; an aberration brought about by the novelty of glamorous and exotic surroundings and the attentions of important men like her father; a deviation from the carefully planned course on which he had initially set himself. He had also become extraordinarily touchy once he was a father, probably due to over-conscientiousness allied to inexperience, though, in this too, there were signs that he regretted what they had done. He had been adamant that Maya should be given a secure identity, be given time to put down firm roots, not be bothered by the accident of her parentage. She had been five years old before he allowed her to be taken to stay with her grandparents in Bombay. Badly affected by the climate and the food, she had been seriously unwell and the memory of all this, reinforced by her father's attitude, which she did not understand but which entered her consciousness by osmosis, had made her unwilling to go again.

At quite a young age she had become aware of the way in which both her mother's looks and her own sometimes confused people. They sometimes confused her. There had been other Indian children in her school, and she realised that if she was not quite like her English friends, she was not exactly like them either.

"Well, darling," Soshan had tried to explain, "there are all kinds of people in India with many different languages and religions. I am a Parsi. We came, hundreds of years ago, from Persia, the country we now call Iran, and we have our own beliefs and customs but though we appear a little different, we are definitely Indians."

Maya, desperately trying to define herself and bewildered by these additional complexities, had refused to listen or learn more about any of this and her fight to hold on to her chosen view of herself as totally English made her a prickly, independent spirit. Soshan had been accustomed to children who, even in modern times, were obedient by western standards but, driven not only by sympathy but by a recognition of her own responsibility for Maya's difficulties, had allowed her considerable leeway. This only led to more clashes with Peter, an authoritarian and surprisingly old-fashioned father.

"It's pure laziness, Soshan. You can't make the effort to discipline her. I put up with a degree of domestic discomfort but where Maya is concerned you really must take more trouble."

Soshan shifted in her seat and adjusted her earplugs as if she could somehow shut out the remembered coldness of his voice. Throughout this slow erosion of all she had so naively imagined that they felt for each other, their battles over parenting had become a substitute for all the other quarrels between them. Yet, in the end, all that survived was a bleak conviction that having a child imposed a duty on them to continue to live together.

Maya had known precisely what was going on and become sullen and rebellious in response, doing everything she could to annoy and worry both parents but finding ever more subtle ways of venting her hostility on her mother, constantly finding fault with her clothes, her way of talking to people, her cooking and the vaguely oriental and formal decor that she favoured.

"Why does everything have to be so foreign? My friends' houses are so much more comfortable. Ours is like a museum. And when they come here, you always sit down and talk to them. They don't come here to talk to you. Oh! I just wish you were a proper mother!"

That heartfelt cry, echoing and re-echoing over the years, across the void of separation, was still an unhealed wound. Scar tissue had formed but it was best to avoid pressing on it. Underneath it was still raw. And this, apparently, had been Maya's final judgement. Their last disastrous meeting had not changed anything.

Most people, her parents particularly, felt it very odd that she had gone for so long with so little contact with her daughter. It embarrassed them. Soshan was beyond embarrassment. Never having dealt with conflict before meeting Peter, the misery of finding disapproval where she had always known loving approbation had taught her to prefer the easy way out in testing situations. By staying away from Maya she was admittedly avoiding confrontation but, in allowing her to dictate the terms of engagement, was not being totally cowardly but accepting her own guilt. It seemed right that because of her failure as a wife and mother she should do penance. Despite her frustration and disappointment, she even felt that her recent attempt to ambush Maya had justifiably failed.

She was roused from such gloomy thoughts when her neighbour tapped her gently on the arm and she saw that a stewardess was offering them breakfast. She removed her earplugs, pulled down the table in front of her and accepted her meal.

"I hope you don't mind my waking you like that." Sitting next to her was a small, elderly Indian woman whom she had briefly acknowledged as they had found their seats after boarding. "They take so long to serve any food and I felt sure you would need something to eat by now."

"Thank you. I wasn't actually asleep. I just had my eyes closed. And, yes, I am ready for some food. I certainly need some liquid and often the juice that they give you with breakfast is the best part of what they give you all day."

The social niceties over, they both ate in silence. Soshan had barricaded herself into solitude at the start of the journey but as she finished eating and pushed away her tray, dreaded a return to her thoughts and still felt unequal to her book. It was a very modern and conflicted novel and, in the mood she had induced in herself, an inappropriate choice. More than half inclined for conversation, she discreetly examined her fellow traveller whom she judged to be in her mid-sixties, a neat if rather matronly figure dressed in a simple cotton sari. Her face was broad, only lightly wrinkled and, though quite dark-skinned, had that faded, rather dusty look that such complexions take on with age. Her iron grey hair was drawn back in a severe bun. But there was nothing severe about her general demeanour. She looked serene and kindly. Soshan gave her a tentative smile.

Her implied invitation was eagerly taken up. "Are you on your way to India for a holiday or are you returning from one?" The little woman wrinkled her nose in mock dismay. "Oh dear, I'm sorry. It's hard to believe, but I have lived for nearly forty years in England without losing any of my Indian nosiness."

"That's a harsh word!" Soshan raised her eyebrows. "To answer your question, I'm returning from a short business trip to London. I did live in England at one time, though, and my experience there would incline me to be kinder about what you describe as nosiness. Let's call it sociable curiosity. And I have my share of that. You say you've spent years in England. That doesn't sound as if you were born there. So, where exactly do you come from? South India somewhere? Kerala maybe?"

"Ah! How good to be with someone who can see me in all my fine, regional detail. I've grown used to being merely an Indian. I wouldn't go so far as to say that to my English friends all Indian faces are the same, but they do have a rather generalised picture of us. Yes, I am originally from Kerala. You, I think, are a Parsi. And for you, Bombay must be home."

"Home? For us inter-cultural wanderers that is a loaded word. But yes, I am a Parsi and, in essence, that is what Bombay is for me. It's where I was born, where I now live. But I have an ex-husband and a daughter in England and if I'm totally honest – and on a plane, with a compatriot whom I may never meet again, why not take a chance to be honest – there is a part of me that has really tried, but never managed, to see that as home. I'm sorry. You don't want to hear all this. I am imposing on you. I've spent too long this morning thinking about my life and I have lost my sense of decency."

"My dear, please don't think like that. I know exactly what you mean by such a feeling of displacement. I also understand just how easy it is, in our situation, to confide in a familiar-looking stranger. I am, by the way, a doctor, a medical doctor, so I am very used to confidences and you are not imposing at all. And let's not give up on each other so early or think we might never see each other again. Every meeting should be potentially the start of a friendship if we are to make the most of life. Perhaps we should at least exchange names. I'm Mariam Thomas. Dr Thomas. A Christian, as you will realise from my name. A Christian who threw herself to the lions because that was the way she saw herself able to fully use her talents." She gave a small snort. "Sorry. I'm always too ready to play with words. The NHS, where I started my career and in which I still work doesn't, even in its current incarnation, deserve to be likened to a lion's den. To be serious, I'm a lonely, exiled spinster who has lived and worked abroad for many years and whose work is her life. I'm making a rare return to my native town for a wedding. I'm staying in Bombay – the habits of a lifetime clearly prevent us both from calling it Mumbai – for a few days with a nephew who is also a doctor and then I'm off to Kerala. There! I've confided in you, so now we start on equal terms."

"You are very kind. I'm Soshan Fielding. My husband, as you may have gathered, was English and that was my married name. My maiden name was Sethna. Since my divorce, I have lived alone in a small flat in my parent's building and they do a great deal for me. In material terms it has almost been a return to girlhood but of course there can be no such emotional return."

"No. We were probably both too young and green when we started out to realise that in choosing our new lives we were off on a one-way journey. How could we have been anything but inexperienced? It was such a leap into the void. There is no preparation for that."

"How was it for you in England, to begin with? You must have been very lonely. I had my husband and then my child and I was still often lonely."

"Of course I was homesick but there was my work and that was what really counted. It was my reason for being there."

"I've read about the prejudice there could be in those days. Did it affect you?"

"Well, my dear, to be totally frank – as I feel that I can be with you – there will always be prejudice. It's part of our human DNA. Not necessarily racial prejudice, more tribal I would say. Generally, people are most comfortable with people who are like themselves. I seem to have met three types overall. There is a hard core of those who will never be reconciled to foreigners. In England, in the early days, they were the ones who dared to ask not to be treated by me. Now, they submit, but I sense a deep internal withdrawal in them, as if the touch of my brown hand might blister their fair skin." Mariam put the said hand over her mouth. "I'm sorry, that sounds so bitter and I'm not bitter at all. Perhaps I'm reverting to my younger, less tolerant self. Fortunately, to off-set such unpleasantness, I meet another delightful set of people who simply don't see difference, who are always open to everyone as a friend. Then there are the vast majority who just appear accepting. They have learned acceptance. I have to say, though, that in the attics of their minds they have stored away some old prejudices like valuable, old-fashioned heirlooms and, unfortunately, modern day events are encouraging some of them to bring these down again and dust them off." She paused and added apologetically, "Forgive me. I'm becoming an old bore. I didn't mean to make a speech."

They could not have explained why they had so quickly overcome all possible barriers. Both were obviously by inclination rebels and, suspended literally between the two worlds they inhabited, perhaps felt unconstrained by the rules of either. Though they took short, quiet breaks for further meals, for the odd nap, or simply a rest from talking, they had told each other a great deal more before their journey was over and had optimistically exchanged addresses and promises to keep in touch. They both knew that such instant affinities do not always lead any further as life takes hold of one, but in the arrival hall, Mariam gave a last confirming wave from the midst of the vociferous group who had come to greet her and Soshan, with a nod, moved away to where her driver was waiting for her.

There was no-one else there and, fighting against all the sadness and sense of failure that this unfulfilling trip had aroused, she was actually glad of this as it would mean not having to answer any questions. She shouldered her way through the hot and heaving hubbub, fending off over-eager porters, assailed by the cloying scent of welcome garlands and the echoing roar of large numbers of people shouting excitedly and emphatically. This latter had a reassuring lilt and remembered rhythms that she found comforting. Outside the airport building she breathed in the humid, aromatic air and already felt her hair damp against the back of her neck, but a large, air-cooled car and a trusted servant were waiting for her. She could relax and rely on others to look after her. She pushed away any thoughts of disappointment. Whatever she had said about the ambiguities of a return or the impossibility of defining home for a wanderer like herself, something very deep inside her, like a small, restless animal, sighed and settled down contentedly.

FIVE

Monday is not a usually a day for introspection. It is a day that pulls everyone still anchored to earth back to routine and reality. On the farm, Robert rose at six and went about his usual duties. At the cottage, Joyce did the household chores, dealt with her poultry, added more eggs to the bowl in the conservatory and, in the afternoon, got down to some serious gardening.

At eight fifteen, John and Maya drove to Cambridge, left the car in their designated space outside a tall, modern building on the outskirts of the university area and parted after entering its revolving door. He used an identity card to access the lift to the laboratories on the first and second floors and she went into the offices that opened directly off the lobby. They would not see each other until the evening. To make sharing this workplace viable, they had made it a rule not to meet for lunch. The laboratory personnel, whose times were, in any case, somewhat irregular, mostly ate in a canteen allocated to them on the higher floor of their segregated area, while the office staff, if they did not eat at their desks, either went to a pub or took packed lunches out into a small, near-by park.

Maya had been astonished and grateful to find how comfortable she was during the time she spent here. For eight hours, every Monday to Friday, the anxiety, the dissatisfaction, the restlessness that had plagued her since childhood and, because she was unable to trust her luck, had only been partially assuaged by her marriage, never troubled her. Her co-workers were a mixed group of men and women in their twenties and thirties who, though not un-ambitious, were not driven go-getters. They floated easily through a working day that left them plenty of energy to enjoy the agreeable social round that Cambridge offered and they floated equally easily in and out of friendships, as staff came and went, picking up the essentials about one another but not asking too many probing questions. Floating, particularly in punts, was very much an accepted Cambridge activity. In idle, reflective moments, Maya liked to imagine herself as a reclining figure in the centre of such a boat, gliding along a narrow, tree-lined river, making progress without making much effort. It seemed an apt metaphor for her office life.

"It's a bit chilly for the park, today. We're off to the pub, Maya. Are you coming?" At one o'clock, her colleagues were gathering bags and jackets and moving off towards the lobby.

She found her own bag and followed them out of the building. They walked in a straggle of twos and threes through the pale sunshine. It was a day that had gone back on the warm promise of the weekend. There was a brisk wind and the temperature had dropped considerably. Hearing a jet somewhere overhead, she looked up and saw a scattering of high cloud in an almost colourless sky. Somewhere above more distant clouds her mother was in midflight, probably a model of glamorous sophistication engaging vivaciously with fellow travellers. She shook off this irritating image. The aircraft she was looking for, only made real by a belated roar

46

and a faint and diminishing trail, was gone before it could even be located. She felt a rush of relief that any immediate threat to her new life had fortunately, if temporarily, similarly vanished.

"Come on Maya. What are you dawdling for? You're daydreaming." The others were already holding the door of the pub open and looking back to where she loitered, gazing upwards, her eyes half-closed against the glare. She hurried to join them as they pushed their way through a noisy, pulsating crowd to where an advance couple had already occupied two tables and covered several chairs with bags and jackets as markers of their captured territory.

Ordering lunch and passing the correct food to the correct person was a chaotic affair. "Who wanted a burger?" "Hey! Those are my chips." "Whose pork pie is this?" "Who is having the pizza?" It was about fifteen minutes before Maya was handed the sandwich and lager she had asked for. These lunches, supposedly a respite from routine, were not in the least restful. Conversation was a strain on the throat and the ears and, if pressed, she could not have explained why she enjoyed them, but she drank her frothy lager, played her small part in the equally frothy chatter and returned to the office and an afternoon of concentrated work as if her identity had in some way been validated.

As she sat down at her desk she felt a slight nausea. It was odd. She had only eaten a sandwich. Perhaps the lager had been a mistake. She drank a glass of water and felt a little better but half an hour later an intense wave of heat flushed through her followed by what felt like a draught moving up her back. She shivered and turned from hot to cold. The room seemed to be darkening and the desk in front of her receding. Her eyes were heavy, she was seeing everything as if through a smaller and smaller opening and she fell forward.

"Maya! Maya! Here, lean on me." She was vaguely aware of voices. "Maya, put your head down on your knees. It's no good, she can't hear me. Someone bring a glass of water. Get some ice from the water cooler. "

"Is that a good idea? She's sweating and her forehead is wet but she's icy cold."

"It looks bad. I think we need to get help."

Maya slowly raised her head and half opened her eyes but did not appear to be focusing on anything. Then, once again she fell forward and began to draw rasping breaths.

"Hold her head up. She can't breathe because her neck is constricted."

"Maya! Can you hear me, Maya?"

Someone drew out a phone and said hesitantly, "I think I should call the paramedics."

One of the girls was now holding Maya's head up as directed and sponging her forehead with rolled up tissues soaked in water while the others were fluttering round her in a largely helpless way. Then, after several anxious minutes, she opened her eyes fully and looked at them all rather blearily. This time, within a few seconds, she sat up straight and spoke quite clearly.

"It's alright. I just felt odd for some reason. I'm fine now."

The girl against whom she had been leaning, looked round. "Perhaps it's best not to make that call." She rubbed Maya's back gently. "Are you sure you feel stronger, Maya? You gave us a terrible fright. We were going to call the medics but if you are sure you really are alright perhaps we shouldn't bother them."

"No, don't. I'm honestly better. It was just a faint. Perhaps it was something in my lunch. I'll just sit still for a while and then things can go back to normal."

"That sort of faint wasn't normal. It's not as though you are ill or have had any particular weaknesses. Since we've known you, you've always been really fit. You've never had any time off or anything. You can't just pretend this hasn't happened. We'll call John and let him know."

"There's no need for that. I don't want to interrupt his work. If I can rest for a while, I'll be perfectly okay."

"We can't risk another scare. You must go home." Their office manager, a tall, elegant woman in her mid-fifties, had been called and now arrived to take command. "Your husband must be told that you are unwell and you can decide together what to do about getting you checked by a doctor. We can't take that responsibility." She surveyed the open work area critically. "If you feel able, we'll go to my office. You can wait for him there. It's quieter and more private."

She led Maya to a comfortable chair in her glassed-in cubicle and seeing John coming through the general area, walked out to meet him. After a short, muted conversation, she tactfully went off, leaving them alone together. John came in and stood looking down at Maya, concerned but calm.

"What is all this about? Are you feeling strong enough to get to the car and cope with the journey back? If so, I think we'll leave the post mortems until later. You have caused a bit of an upheaval here and we don't want to disrupt things any longer. I've arranged with your boss for you to have a day off tomorrow. I've taken one too and we can then see how things go."

Maya felt weak in a quite different way at the sight of him, longing to feel his arms round her but knowing better than to expect any public demonstration.

"I'm fine. Really. It was just a spell of dizziness. It could be what I ate for lunch. You're right. I don't want any more fuss here. Let's go."

The drive was quick and easy – at this time there was far less traffic – but she sat with her eyes closed. She was better but looking out of the window and becoming aware of motion still made her a little giddy. John glanced across anxiously at her from time to time but did not say anything. Once they were indoors, he drew her to him and, still without speaking, rested his cheek on the top of her head and held her close for several minutes before he stood back and examined her closely.

"Now, I want you to go and sit down and I'll bring you some tea. Then we have to talk. I don't think you are seriously ill but there is definitely *something* serious that needs putting right." As Maya started to speak, he put his finger on her lips. "No. Don't say anything. Just sit and wait. Whatever problem you.... we.... have, we need to take our time to sort it out."

He went off to the kitchen, came back with a tray and passed her a cup of tea. He watched her over the rim of his own as she drank it. Then putting both cups back on the tray, he set it aside and pulled his chair closer. He reached for her hands, held them in a firm clasp and looked gravely at her.

"I haven't said anything more about what happened between you and your mother. I was ready to leave any discussion of that until you were willing to tell me all the things that you are clearly keeping from me." He gently touched her stricken face. "It's alright. I can take a lot from you, Maya. Even secrecy! But I was shocked by the way you behaved on Saturday. It showed that you have much darker secrets than I had thought possible. This unexplained faint of yours may be a coincidence but I don't think so. That whole episode was extremely stressful and must have taken its toll on you." He again put a finger on her lips as she tried to interrupt him. "No! I don't want to hear what you have to say yet. It's time that I told you what I feel. I see more than you think but there's still far too much hidden inside you. It must be bad for you and it is certainly bad for us." He released her and sat back in his chair for a second as if exhausted and then bent forward. "I know you have explained that things were traumatic for you as a child and that you did not want to have much to do with your parents. I went along with that. I went along with our almost secretive wedding though it hurt my mother and puzzled my relatives and, I have to say, puzzled me. It probably laid up problems with them all that could have been avoided. It's time that you were honest and told me a great deal more about what troubles you than you have so far. I've met both your parents now, if under less than ideal conditions, and they will quite reasonably expect *some* contact with me. Why are you so afraid of that?"

Maya now reached out for his hands and clung on to them, her eyes shuttered and her body tense as if she were confronting some fearful, internal image. "So much went wrong when I was a child that I can't really recall things in any sensible, coherent way. I'm always terrified of letting you find out just how messed up I am. Afraid I'll lose you. If you knew my parents better you would see how this all started. I don't want you to know them. I don't want us to be touched by all that misery." Her voice was high and her grip tightened. She stared unseeingly over his shoulder. "My father never wanted any connection with India beyond his one short posting there and my mother hated living in England but they had chosen each other. I used to think how much in love they must have been in the beginning to ignore all that. Yet I saw them acting as if they detested each other. You don't know how beastly they could be when they fought. I was young but not too young to learn from them that love doesn't necessarily last. It isn't always enough. When they finally admitted to themselves what a mistake they had made, they used me as a weapon against each other. They no longer thought about me or cared about me." She met his eyes and hers were wide and over-bright. "The other night, after the call from Mother, I woke up feeling as if grief had seeped into every crack of my body, that if I cried forever I'd still never use up all my unshed tears. I saw you sleeping so calmly beside me. I desperately wanted you to stay that way. I'm calm on the outside.... most of the time.... in daylight. But if I let you see what is churning round inside me, if you find out how I have behaved sometimes, you, too, might find it impossible to care about me....to love me."

John freed himself from her convulsive grasp and put his arms round her. She rested against his shoulder and, finally, wept. He let her weep for a while and then he raised her head and brushed his fingers gently over her wet cheeks. "Don't cry. I won't ever stop loving you. I didn't rush into this, Maya. I'm not the impulsive sort. I didn't pretend that there were no complications when I met you. I don't want to upset you by talking about this because I know how it weighs on you, but I admit I was worried that my family might find it hard to deal with your background. I come from a pretty staid lot. But I soon realised that I didn't care about them or anyone. All I cared about was you. And that won't change, I promise."

She pulled away from him. "I want to believe that. But I do get frightened. Most of the time, it seems to me that if I ignore the past, if you never know about it, it can't harm us. Then something comes up, like Mother wanting to see us, and it all comes flooding back. It's as if I'm a child again, hearing those furious voices or, even worse, my father's voice so cold and cutting and my mother crying. I was usually in bed when they had their worst arguments but I'd creep out onto the landing and listen, hoping to hear them make up and be friends. At first they often did. Later, it usually ended in a horrible silence and they hardly talked to each other for days. As I grew older they were less careful about making sure I didn't hear them fight. It happened at any time. And it was more and more often about me. How they should treat me. How I should be brought up. There was always this thing about England and India. That was there from the beginning. Mother missed Bombay and, when she felt really homesick, she'd lash out and say horrible things about England; the country and the people. How did she suppose that made me feel? My father is a very driven man. I'm sure that all he really cares about is his work and over the years, as he's become wealthier and more successful, that's simply got worse. I realise now that going to India was part of his drive to succeed. He wasn't interested in the country. He didn't even like it. I think that while he was there, he had a mad moment over my mother and then, when he came back to what really mattered to him, he couldn't put up with the distraction of dealing with her unhappiness." Maya's face contorted and her tone was bitter. "Maybe he thought that she would put him first and be a traditional, docile housewife. You've seen her. That wasn't going to happen."

She stopped abruptly but, just as John was about to say something, went on sadly, "I can understand how hard it must have been for her. But she shouldn't have let it stop her from thinking about me. My grandmother had occasionally looked after me when I was a baby and after Mother went off, she looked after me again, staying with Dad or having me to stay with her for school holidays. But she was old. She didn't understand how much everything had changed since she was young. She couldn't really help me. And it was awful to realise she thought that, by caring for me, she was finally getting back at my mother and showing her up. They all used me." She thumped the arm of her chair. "Why didn't my mother stay in England with me? If she'd been a proper mother she wouldn't have let me go through all that, put herself first."

She buried her face in her hands but as John tried to hold her again, she raised her head and pushed him away. She looked quite fierce and her tone was defiant. "There's worse. The really terrible thing is that they made me behave badly. I deliberately tried not to do well at school because I knew how important that was to them. I even played truant, disappearing for whole days and driving them frantic. When all that got me in trouble with my teachers, I stopped. I realised that I wanted to succeed for my own sake. The thing is that because of all the hassle and worry I never did as well as I knew I could, in class or in exams. That made me angry too. Then, when I was fourteen, they obviously felt that I didn't need them to pretend anymore and they divorced. Mother wanted to take me to India. She simply didn't think about how that would be for me. I'd only been there once, and that when I was very young. I had very hazy ideas about it and I didn't know my grandparents at all. She didn't even consider that she would be taking me to a foreign country and ripping up my whole life. So I refused to go even for holidays. I wanted her to see just how furious she'd made me. Next, I got back at my father by passing up a last minute chance to go to university and that hurt me as much as it hurt him. I spent a year or so doing a whole lot of piddling little jobs and brought a few so-called boyfriends back to the house, all as unsuitable as they could be. I really hated myself. Then I thought, 'I'm a grown-up. I don't need parents anymore. The best thing to do is to get right away.' Because I felt that my father should at least give me physical shelter, I stayed with him while I took my secretarial course but I looked online for jobs as far away as possible. I found this one in Cambridge and I met you." Her lips quivered and her eyes brimmed again. "I don't want either of them to come into our life and bring all that anger, all that failure with them, those battles over where I belong, which country is best. I want a normal English life, a peaceful life of my own with you." She was shivering slightly, worn down by this outpouring, this release of years of repressed pain and panic.

John stood up. "Come here." As she got out of her chair and came over to him, he wound his arms round her and said in a shaky voice, "You will have that life. It won't be a fairy tale but it *will* be a case of living happily ever after, I promise you. We won't escape the ups and downs that hit everyone but we'll always be at peace with each other." He hesitated, took a deep breath and said seriously, "I won't rush you but, if you really want a quiet life, if we are to be completely at peace, we will have to find a way for you to let your parents back into our life without being afraid that they can spoil it."

She tried to break free but he held on to her and rested his forehead against hers. "Really Maya, it is something we have to do. You will always be haunted by them if we don't. They are ghosts that have to be laid."

SIX

On the internet a broad blue line, like an enticing, imaginary river heading out to sea, marks the route from Cambridge to Aldeburgh. Following this along what is, in reality, the very unromantic and traffic clogged A14, John and Maya were heading for the Suffolk coast. This was a spur of the moment expedition decided on over a late breakfast, in response to yet another bright, if windy, summer day and at the urging of Maya, who had argued persuasively that since they had already decided on a likely reason for her health problem they should temporarily forget it. If John was right and stress and anxiety had brought it on, then surely a better cure for it than a fraught session on the phone and a depressing wait in the local surgery would be a complete change of scene and a few hours of total freedom.

This chance of a day together with no pre-planned chores or duties had come about so unexpectedly, a welcome holiday despite its cause, that she had been jolted into a realisation of how quickly and unthinkingly they had fallen into an unvarying, almost middle-aged, routine: Monday to Friday working in Cambridge; Saturday spent on housework and shopping, with the reward of an occasional evening outing; Sunday spent in Hadleigh with Joyce. It had all apparently fallen into place inevitably because everything that they did was something that *had* to be done. John was a natural doer of what had to be done, while she had always, even in her rebellious and provocative teens, longed for stability and regularity, but it had not been inevitable. They had been married just six months. It should have been a carefree, creative time. They should have been adjusting to each other, exploring joint ways of thinking about things, finding new ways of doing things and, even better, finding new things to do. Instead they had been over-cautious and nervous; she concealing her inner self and John navigating around her, skilfully avoiding any confrontation or controversy. Her unexplained faint had been a necessary catalyst. It had forced her into the open and made her reveal the fears, the sorrow that had been festering inside her, a metaphorical tumour that should never have been allowed to twist their relationship into something so hesitant and, it now had to be admitted, unsatisfactory. Just how unsatisfactory had become clear to her when, after their bruising talk had brought them much closer, she had experienced something rather more passionate than John's usual, gentle, protective affection.

She had woken that morning to find herself moulded to the shape of his back, sweating slightly, one side of her face pressed against his neck. As she stirred, he had moved slowly away from her and sat up, rubbing his eyes, but when she reached out and stroked his arm, rolled back on his side and bent over to give her a long kiss. This time she had been the one to break away and sit up.

"The sun is streaming through the blinds. What on earth is the time?"

"Nearly eight o'clock. I think we wore ourselves out last night." He gave her a slanting look, a new gleam in his eyes. "It must have been all that talking."

That he dared to half joke about what had so very recently been intensely serious and caused so much heartache was a measure of how much things had changed in a few hours. Trying to look stern, she stood up quickly but sat down heavily again and said rather faintly, "I feel a bit dizzy."

John had come round to her and felt her forehead. "You are a bit clammy. Is this how you were yesterday?"

"It's not the same. I don't feel nearly so bad and it's already passing."

"Well, anyway, I'm going to phone and try to get you an appointment with the doctor. It will be best to get this sorted out."

In the end she had won that argument and here they were, just passing the heath and paddocks of Newmarket on the way to Bury St. Edmunds, where they might stop briefly on their way back but which they would now bypass in favour of a planned arrival in Aldeburgh in time for a leisurely lunch and an afternoon walk on the beach, all their worries to be temporarily blown away by a sea breeze.

They had pictured themselves eating in one of the hotels that they had found online, hotels with large elegant dining rooms that overlooked the shoreline, but as they drove into the town it was already a little later than they had planned and one of the first things that they saw was a fish and chip shop. With hunger sharpened by the very inviting smell wafting around the streets and overpowering any scent of the sea, fish and chips were what they settled on. They took them, wrapped in paper and placed in a plastic bag, to eat outside in the sunshine, in defiance of greasy fingers and the unexpectedly sharp breeze that had hit them once they left the car. Moving out from the shelter of the town buildings towards the sea was, in fact, like entering some huge wind-tunnel whose sound filled their heads like a sort of atmospheric tinnitus.

"I feel like Alice in Wonderland." Maya cupped her hands round her mouth and turned to John.

"Like who?" He bent towards her as her words were whipped away across the vast expanse of sea and sky. He shook his head and pulled her over to a pair of fishing boats drawn up on the sand. They sat down, breathless, under the side of one of these and the roar and the pull of the wind died away. "Like who?"

"Like Alice in Wonderland. Look out there. It's an enormous space. I feel as if I have suddenly shrunk to a miniature size."

"Well let's fill you up with these delicious things. Wasn't there something in that story labelled 'Eat me'? And didn't Alice grow larger?" John passed her a steaming package. "So, eat this and then you'll grow back to normal again."

They ate voraciously, uninhibitedly like children, and after this picnic, removed their shoes, rolled up their jeans and, paddling out into the surf, washed away the last sticky, clinging crumbs of batter from their faces and fingers. The piercing cold of the water cut through any post lunch heaviness and there was an onshore north-easterly intent on scouring them totally clean. Invigorated, eager to walk, they faced into it and set off along the beach.

"It's a bit crunchy." Maya found it a little disappointing. It was not the smooth golden curve, soft beneath her feet that holiday advertising had imprinted on her brain but a rather grey, messy stretch of sand and shingle. Then, as she succumbed to a beachcombing urge and walked with her head down, concentrating on only a small area of ground in front of her, she discovered that the endless pebbles, so painful underfoot, were like a cache of spectacular mini artworks, blue-veined in a variety of designs, as if scattered there by some giant craftsman specialising in Batik. They were entrancing. She kept darting forward in a compulsive search for more and different shapes and patterns, constantly coming back to John with her palms held out to display particularly interesting finds. They walked on and on, leaving the town and most other walkers behind them. Only as they at last turned back did Maya raise her head, begin to look around and enjoy the wider seascape, the sunshine and the exhilarating sensation of her hair streaming wildly around her.

"It's quite magical here. It's not as I imagine the seaside. It's much wilder. No pier, no candy floss, no donkeys. It is absolutely the right place for us today. Being made to feel small is just what I needed and walking in this wind is like going through a cleansing process, whirled inside a sort of marine washing machine." She danced around John, repeating 'marine machine, marine machine' in a gleeful chorus.

Watching her, John felt something hard and hot inside his chest. His eyes stung and it was not because of the wind. He had a momentary vision of a small child with wide, dark eyes and long, dark hair, dancing across the beach; Maya as a child, the child she should have been, not that scared little thing huddled on a landing with her arms round herself as a defence against frightening, angry adult voices. He reached out and tried to hold her but she gave him a passing tap on the arm and eluded him.

He shook his head at her. "What's got into you suddenly?"

"The wind. It's rushing through me. I feel so light and free."

"Well all this has certainly done you good in more ways than one."

Coming up beside him she leaned in and rested her head on his shoulder for a second. "I certainly feel good. Thank you for a wonderful day."

They were now getting back to a part of the beach where there were other walkers and they became suddenly sedate. Hand in hand and happy in a simpler, more carefree way than had seemed possible yesterday, they made their way slowly back to the car.

In the office the next morning, Maya was welcomed back with little fuss. This small, contained world had moved on. Even the previous day's events were already filed away. She, too, wanted to go forward and forget what had happened. Getting dressed that morning she had felt a momentary giddiness but it had quickly passed and she was determinedly ignoring the lethargy that had replaced the euphoria of the previous day. She thought it must be caused by waking to mundane reality after a day of glorious freedom.

At midmorning though, as she and one of the girls were standing alone at the coffee machine, she was overcome by a wave of weakness and had to lean against the wall for a moment.

Her colleague said hesitantly, "Have you thought that you might be pregnant, Maya? My sister has been having faints and dizzy spells like yours and she's just found out that she is." As Maya turned a startled face, she added. "It's not impossible is it? It's not hard to find out. You could do a home test. You get them at any chemist."

Maya guiltily recalled recent moments of carelessness. She had not taken the obvious into account, had not, until now, considered any such likelihood. She was totally unprepared for it and had no idea how to respond emotionally to the thought of pregnancy but, clearly, however remote a possibility, now that it had been put to her she must act. She wouldn't rely on self-diagnosis. She would overcome her reluctance and visit the surgery. Feeling better again, however, she put off doing anything. It was always such an effort to set up an appointment and seeing the doctor always involved so much wasted time, so much waiting about. It was simpler to let things slide. Five days later, waking to terrible stomach cramps and nausea, she discovered that she was bleeding heavily and that this delay had been unwise. Now she had no choice.

The doctor, a middle-aged woman, confirmed that she was pregnant and having a miscarriage but spoke calmly and reassuringly. This was not unusual in these early stages and no great cause for worry. She must take things easy and should come in to the surgery immediately if there were any further symptoms in the next few hours. In any event, an appointment would be arranged for her at the hospital the following day for a scan and possibly an internal examination. A second one might also be necessary. They would keep her under observation for a time but it was unlikely that a surgical intervention would be called for. Usually in such cases, the situation resolved itself naturally and if it did so without complications, as was most probable, she should be careful for a while and then carry on with her life as usual. These things happened; she was young; she would almost certainly conceive again and, almost equally certainly, with a happier outcome.

They had never talked about children, had not really talked much at all. They had actually known each other for quite a short time and this, like much else, had been left un-examined, un-discussed, as if the mere fact of managing the perceived differences that could have separated them and dealing with the doubts of others about those was enough to be getting on with. She had no idea of what John was thinking or feeling but was disturbed by her own reactions. They seemed unnatural. Struggling with the unpleasant demands of her body, she had not thought much about the cause of such misery or been aware of anything beyond immediate physical discomfort. The crisis over, she decided rather bleakly that she had failed in some important way and this reignited some of her earlier anxieties. Her fear that John might find her unlovable flared up again and nagged at her. More frightening was her lack of any deeper more mature response. The lost baby had been so unplanned, she had been so unaware of it and it had so little real identity, so little actuality, for her that she could not summon up grief. This felt like a further inadequacy.

John allowed no time for any probe into his state of mind. He was intent on action. As soon as most of her hospital checks were completed and everything was seen, as predicted, to have resolved naturally, he swept her up in hasty preparations for a week's stay with his mother. It was impossible to tell him that she shrank from the thought of living closely with Joyce for so many days but also unthinkable to appear to criticise her by pointing out that she might be equally reluctant to be forced into such prolonged intimacy with a not entirely welcome daughter-in-law. A mild suggestion that she would be better at home and near her doctor was brushed aside. He was adamant.

"You need a complete rest. You must take at least a week. I have to go into work and I shall feel easier if you are with someone who will look after you. Hadleigh is the perfect answer. You will be quiet and well looked after. Mother's neighbour and friend is a doctor and he could always be called on for any medical emergency."

Maya, seeing how concerned he was about every detail of her care and well-being, was ashamed of having used a hint about being near a doctor as a blatant tactic to get her own way. She saw absolutely no need of one and had an inner conviction that it was over and there would be no further horrors, no more indignities, no prods and probes to be endured beyond a final check-up booked for the Friday afternoon. With John decreeing that she needed a further day after this to ensure that she was absolutely fit to travel, they would leave on Sunday morning and spend the usual day together at the cottage before John left her there. She had to fit in with these arrangements without any overt reluctance. She braced herself for a difficult week and began to gather together what she needed to pack.

She listened in as John called his mother but could not make out from his side of the conversation what Joyce might be saying. One thing she knew. She and Joyce had been silently and unsuccessfully trying to find a way towards each other for his sake all these months. Perhaps at their last meeting Joyce had made more effort than ever before, and she herself was seeing things in a more open-minded way, but now they were to be forced to undergo a tougher and possibly decisive test. She would find out if her good intentions of changing and being more considerate and mature could be put into practice.

SEVEN

Soshan was woken as usual at seven by the sound of a tea tray being set down on her bedside table. Her bedroom was cool and dark, an air-conditioner and thick blinds cutting out the heat and clamour of the city outside, creating an artificial oasis in which she rested for a few more sleepy minutes before sitting up and greeting a small, barefooted woman in a printed cotton dress who, having dealt with the tea things, was gathering up clothes left strewn over a chair the previous night and putting them into a linen bag to be taken off for washing.

"Good morning, Mary. You can open the curtains, but only a little. I didn't get to sleep until very late. I can't take too much glare."

"Doctor Wadia stayed long time after dinner?"

The two women's eyes met in complete understanding. Mary moved over to the window, partially opened the curtains in a way that ensured that the light was not too strong or too directly on Soshan's face and went off into the bathroom with the laundry bag.

Soshan poured a cup of tea and leaned against the pillows of her wide, luxurious bed, sipping it. "I'm not going anywhere this morning," she called out. "I have some letters to write. Tell Swami that I won't need the car and he can take the time to clean it. This afternoon I'll need to send him into town to do a few errands but I think that I will have a quiet day indoors. There's Mother's party this evening. I'll take it easy today."

"Better you have a good breakfast and I make small lunch for you. I am seeing how it is upstairs. So many dishes ordered for party tonight. So much cooking for Ahmed to do. Lucky he is good cook and not lazy. Memsahib awake very, very early this morning. All servants rushing-bushing about already. Important people coming for dinner."

Mary had no inhibitions about speaking freely to Soshan and always brought her this morning report on what her parents and their servants were doing. She had come to work for the Sethnas as a young woman, a Christian from South India, desperately needing both work and a place to live. Now, at nearly sixty, she was so much part of the fabric of their lives that she had no life anywhere else. She had known Soshan since she was a toddler and often treated her as if she were still a girl. When, after her divorce, Soshan had returned to Bombay and moved into this flat, one floor below that of her parents, Mary had moved in with her and, with the help of a boy who was sent down every morning to do the heavy cleaning, managed most of the household chores, including cooking. She had her own room and bathroom in converted quarters behind the kitchen.

With this degree of separation giving Soshan some privacy, while having Mary always on call, they rubbed along together very well. If Mary was something of a go-between, frequently spending time in the family flat chatting to the servants, and if it was sometimes a little irksome to have all her affairs so closely observed, Soshan also found it comforting to have as a confidante and support someone who knew her so well. Mary did not hesitate to criticise her but if anyone else said a word against her was aggressive and uncompromising in her defence. She often took Soshan to task over the matter of her friendship with the doctor who had spent the previous evening here but if this was ever discussed among the other servants, its secrets were totally safe with her and gossips got short shrift.

She now came out of the bathroom and stood beside the bed. "Tea finished? Doctor Wadia coming to party tonight? Memsahib likes him very much."

"Alright, Mary! I already know very well that Mother likes him. No matchmaking this morning. Yes he *is* coming this evening. Now we'll just get on with our day."

"I go get breakfast. I will put it on balcony. Have it before your bath this morning. Get some fresh air before is getting too hot."

Mary marched off with the tray, rather straight-backed and stiff and left Soshan smiling a little ruefully. She knew Mary's hopes for her. She also understood that there was some fear mixed in with these hopes, but that, while half afraid of the upheaval this would cause in their comfortable life, Mary longed for her to have the prestige of a successful marriage and aware of the possibilities offered by the doctor whom they had been talking about, always took every opportunity to plead his cause.

She, too, occasionally dreamed of the life she might have with him. Sohrab Wadia was extremely eligible, a successful surgeon practicing at a reputed hospital and highly respected both within the Parsi community and by all her family and friends. His courtship, if one saw it in these old-fashioned terms, had already somewhat redeemed her in her father's eyes. He was a little older than her, a widower with two daughters, whose wife had died six years earlier. They had been going to concerts, films and parties together for nearly four years and very much enjoyed each other's company. She often visited his flat, had joined him for holidays at a nearby hill-station and occasionally spent weekends with him, his daughters and a group of other friends at a beach bungalow owned by his wealthy father. She realised that no-one could understand why they had not married but, if everyone suspected that they had gone beyond friendship – the shared holidays, regular dinners in her flat and the late hours they kept together there indicating as much – they had now been seen as a couple for so long that the situation was taken for granted and aroused little comment.

Sohrab had, in fact, asked Soshan to marry him but when she had hesitated, appeared to be as content as she was to let things go on as they were for the time being. Both their marriages, in different ways, having ended unhappily, it was, on the whole, convenient and satisfying to live apart while still enjoying the company of someone from the same background and social circle and avoiding solitude and loneliness.

Soshan slid out of bed and ran her hands through her tousled hair. She tried never to think too deeply about her reasons, not so much for refusing as for not immediately accepting his proposal. Her eyes dwelt on the photos of Maya set out on a chest of drawers next to her wardrobe. Why on earth did she keep them there? Each time she looked at them it was like being given a hard blow to her chest. Even now that she knew Maya to be a grown woman with a very agreeable husband, there was no escape from the pain of confronting that childish face, so vulnerable and so wary even in the happiest snapshots.

Sohrab's daughters, Kerman and Persis, were now in their late teens, only a little older than Maya had been at the time of the divorce and the mere fact of them and the loss that they had suffered was another reminder of wrenching separations. She shrank from taking any regular place in their motherless lives. It felt treacherous to Maya and insensitive to them. She got along well enough with them and they were now constantly involved in their own activities, spending more and more time out and about with their friends, but it seemed utterly impossible that she should ever make her part in their family official. She picked up a comb ran it through her unruly hair and, resolutely casting off such thoughts, put on a cotton wrap and went in search of breakfast.

"Everything ready. Omelette and hot chapattis. Mango in fridge for later." Mary came out from the kitchen and watched her go outside and sit at the table.

Some last remnants of greenery around their building made this one of the more desirable locations within the dense, high-rise city and the small, pillared balcony looked down on a well-kept garden with a few slender trees that partially softened the starkness of the towering block of flats opposite. This had erupted ten years ago, cutting off their long cherished view of the sea and raising the decibel level of an already noisy environment, but by carefully placing huge pots of bougainvillea and climbing jasmine at the base of the pillars and around a small dining area, Soshan had created an illusion of privacy and peace. It was still a comparatively restful place to eat, though the endless, raucous altercations of crows, the distant roar of traffic and the inescapable domestic sounds and shrill, penetrating radios in the flats opposite were a constant background reminder of all that lay in wait beyond her personal haven.

Now, in mid July, with the monsoon becoming more sporadic, the air was sultry, almost palpable and even her thin cotton dressing gown was soon clinging to her. Soshan was happy to eat her breakfast outside and give Mary the satisfaction of seeing her supposedly enjoying fresh air but only too glad to go indoors and, after showering and dressing, to retire to the second bedroom in the flat that doubled as her study. There, an air-conditioner shut out both heat and noise and considerably reduced the uncomfortable humidity. She started to deal with some paperwork that, though not urgent, made her feel that she was usefully employed.

That evening the two women went upstairs in the lift together. Soshan was wearing a red silk sari with gold jewellery. Mary wore a crisp white cotton one and her hair, sleek with oil and pulled so tightly back into a knot at the nape of her neck that it almost distorted her features, was adorned with a spray of jasmine. She was always brought in to help out at these gatherings though she did little beyond serving a few snacks and drinks. Soshan hated to think of her alone in the flat below and brought her along to give her a chance to be seen and acknowledged by those old friends among the guests who had known her for years and whose greetings both lifted her spirits and enhanced her status.

As they went in through the open door of the flat, they found that Sohrab, who had called before starting out, was waiting in the hall for them. "You look splendid, Soshan.

Even after our late night." He turned to Mary. "Good evening, Mary. What a wonderful job you do looking after Soshan bai and always keeping her looking so well."

"Not always listening to me though, Doctor ji. You should take care of her too."

Smiling complicitly at each other as she walked jauntily off down the hall, they went through to join the party and Soshan's parents came over to them. They each gave her a dutiful kiss on the forehead. There was never anything in the way that they behaved to suggest any sense of grievance or any particular dissatisfaction with her but they were a little cool and privately never forgot that she had acted rashly and against their advice. If her marriage had turned out well things might have been different but they were always aware of a discarded son-in-law who was almost a stranger to them and a distant granddaughter who showed no wish to see them and who did not even have a good Parsi name. They were grateful that at least it was an Indian name, as her mother had wished, but, apparently for the benefit of her father and the people she lived amongst, a simpler, more anodyne one had been chosen. They did what they could to help their daughter in practical ways but all their attention and affection was concentrated on her two sisters and the four loving and satisfactory grandchildren that they had produced.

Their manner towards Sohrab was markedly warmer and more enthusiastic. Her father clapped him on the shoulder and said, "Come over here, my dear chap. There is someone I particularly want you to meet."

The two men went off together and, as her mother turned to speak to new arrivals, Soshan, left to herself, wandered among the crowd, chatting to her many friends but turning often to where Sohrab stood, his tall, athletic frame slightly inclined and his intense, dark eyes totally focused on anyone he happened to be talking to. Each time she saw him, she felt a rush of affection and a small thrill of pride.

She had already told him about her disastrous meeting with Maya. "I let her think my trip to England was a business affair which was a bit if an exaggeration. I didn't want to scare her off. How sad is that; having to manoeuvre round your own daughter as if setting up a diplomatic mission to a hostile country?"

He had been, as always, sensible and supportive. "It is very distressing for you. I'm lucky with my girls. Things generally go smoothly for us because a traditional background overrides many modern dilemmas and also helped us through the trauma of their mother's death, but there is no guarantee that there won't be storms ahead. There are still boyfriends and marriages to be navigated. Morals and manners everywhere are in a state of flux and these aren't easy matters. Of course it grieves you to be cut off from Maya but maybe when she has children of her own she will be more forgiving and understanding. Don't be too hard on yourself, Soshan. Don't forget that when you went to England, you were younger than Maya is now. You made mistakes. Everyone does. Don't forget, either, that Peter has a lot to answer for. You don't deserve to take all the blame."

"I am Maya's mother. I shouldn't have left her. There is no getting over that hard fact."

"I am only too aware that a mother is usually the most important person in a child's life. But things don't always work out as they should." He shrugged off an uncharacteristic spurt of irritation and resumed quietly, "I don't see what you could have done that would have made things much better. The breakup of a family is going to be devastating no matter how you deal with it. India would have been a foreign country to Maya. Insisting on bringing her here would have verged on cruelty, separating her from all she had grown up with. She wasn't a baby. She was almost an adult. All her ideas and habits were halfway to being formed. Let's suppose you had set up house with her in England. You would have been isolated and miserable. How might that have affected you or Maya?"

"It wouldn't have been ideal but maybe it wouldn't have left her so hurt and bitter."

She knew that what he said was true, that his experience gave him the right to say it, and that rationally she should be less hard on herself. Unfortunately her guilt over Maya was no more subject to reason than her scruples about marrying this delightful man. There was one comfort. Her daughter too had found someone equally decent and agreeable. Soshan really liked John and instinctively trusted him. Perhaps if – when – she could be sure that Maya had a good life with him, she might allow herself to accept Sohrab's proposal and feel it was permissible to take on surrogate daughters.

EIGHT

Sunday morning was grey and depressing from the start and as John and Maya drove to Hadleigh, any memory of the summer sunshine and her upbeat mood of the seaside expedition were washed away and forgotten. There were intermittent flurries of rain and large drops ran down the windscreen like slow tears.

When they drew up at the house and Maya climbed more slowly than usual out of the car, Joyce came out of the conservatory, hurried over and gave her a brief hug. She could not help shrinking from such unexpected physical contact and caught a spark in Joyce's eyes of something that might have been hurt or anger. Her chest tightened in a moment of real panic. How was she going to cope with these next few days? Perhaps she could spend a great deal of time in bed and hide away.

"Maya," John broke in on these unruly thoughts, "just go and sit down. I'll take all your things upstairs and unpack."

"Do you feel like going up and down the stairs, Maya?" Joyce looked at her doubtfully. "I have got your bedroom ready but I thought I'd wait and ask what you'd like to do. I can always make up a bed for you in a corner of the sitting room. It's only a foldout bed but it's very comfortable. I use it there myself, nowadays, when I'm under the weather. It's less trouble to go straight to the kitchen and get a drink in the night if I ever need one. With the new shower I've had installed in the cloakroom, there's now a perfectly serviceable bathroom downstairs."

"Oh Mum! Are you still comfortable here?" John had never considered the implications of the changes that she had made. Suddenly stricken by the thought of her ill and alone, he put down the luggage and threw his arms round her.

"Don't be silly." Joyce freed herself. "We must deal with that stuff. Let's get things sorted and settle Maya in. Where shall we put you, Maya?"

"I'll be alright in the bedroom. There really isn't that much wrong with me now. John is making a fuss. If I'm upstairs, I won't be under your feet all the time."

"If you get under my feet, I've plenty of places where I can get away from you." Joyce was unexpectedly brusque. Then, clearly regretting this lapse and her unfriendly tone, she added, "Well, upstairs it is. Come on John. You stay here, Maya. You can go up later to sort your things."

The day passed, as did all their Sundays, slowly and without excitement. John did one or two small jobs for his mother and they had the usual late and heavy lunch. The only break in the unchanging routine was that after lunch, John insisted Maya should sit quietly and rest while he and his mother went for a walk.

She spent the time that they were away wondering what they wanted to discuss without her. Convinced that this was their real purpose in going off together, she could not stop fretting. She knew she was being childish but she felt on the verge of tears, lonely and left out. "If he wants me to be peaceful and avoid strain," she thought rather peevishly, "this wasn't the best plan." She got up two or three times to look out of the window, to check if they were anywhere in sight and by the time that they finally came back after more than an hour and a half, she was flushed and heavy-eyed.

"I'll go and put the kettle on." Joyce, with a quick look at John, went off to the kitchen.

He sat beside Maya. "I've decided to leave after a cup of Mother's wonder brew. She insists on that. I won't stop for supper. I'll have something when I get back and she will get you a light snack later. Go to bed early. Get as much sleep as possible."

"Don't go yet." She clung to his arm. "Do you realise that I've never spent a night without you since we married. I know it's silly but I feel frightened about coping alone."

"Maya, all you have to do is rest. As to coping, you are capable of anything. You managed before you ever met me, getting employed and housed in Cambridge without help from anyone. I'll be back on Friday. I'll be here for two days before we go home on Sunday."

She drew a small sobbing breath. "What I'm facing now is different from anything I've dealt with before. We've been too caught up in hospitals and treatments. We've avoided talking about what's actually happened to us. It was momentous really, however laid-back we are being about it. Are you sad? Angry? Angry with me? Angry that we've been so careless? I need to know."

John held her chin and made her look at him. "Didn't you promise there would be no more dramas? Of course I'm not angry and I don't think either of us knows yet exactly how sad we are. This has come out of the blue. We haven't thought about children. And this is not the final word on that, in any case. All I do know is that any further physical stress is especially bad for you after the strain you've been under. Just stay here quietly. Get completely well. We'll talk...." he broke off as Joyce came back into the room and there was a slightly awkward silence filled with the setting out of cups and the pouring of tea.

After drinking this he said a quick goodbye. The two women stood side by side as he drove off and continued to stand, not looking at each other or speaking, as he rounded the final bend of the road and was gone. Then Joyce said that she had jobs to do outside; there were a few empty pots to put away that had been left lying around and had filled with rainwater earlier, there were plants to be watered in the greenhouse and her hens had to be fed and shut in.

"You go inside. I like a little potter in the fresh air before I sit down for the evening. I'll be in after about an hour and then I'll get us a bite to eat before you go off to bed. Even if you don't want to sleep so early, the rest will be good for you and you can always read. I've put a small television in your room but perhaps you won't want to be bothered with that. It's mostly rubbish on tonight. There's a lot of rubbish on every night."

Maya, grateful for Joyce's tactful withdrawal and this measure of breathing space, made a real effort when her mother-in-law came back into the house and preparing and eating supper, they managed a friendly chat about inconsequential things. She insisted on helping to clear away and wash up and then both of them were glad for her to go to her room so that they could relax into privacy for the rest of the evening.

She had never been upstairs in the house before but knew that she was sleeping in what had always been set resolutely aside as a guest room. It wasn't exactly fusty but it had an indefinably unused feel to it. All Joyce's bedrooms had remained essentially unchanged since she had first decorated them, long ago, with ornate wallpapers and pale silky curtains in shades, now faded, that picked out the main colours of the birds, butterflies and bunches of flowers rioting over every wall. The beds were high and still covered with valanced bedspreads and matching eiderdowns. Even what was still called John's room had been only slightly modified by the addition of painted bookcases, a sturdier, more serviceable bedcover and heavier curtains and his was the only one that showed signs of wear and tear. A long habit of drawing curtains against the ravages of any sunshine had actually preserved everything remarkably well and, like the rest of the house, the room that Maya now took over demonstrated just what careful, old-fashioned housekeeping could do in any battle against time, dirt and decay.

She sat on a high stool at the mahogany dressing table. On the highly polished wooden top in front of her was a set of old-fashioned silver-backed brushes, a cut-glass oblong tray and two small glass bowls with silver lids. She put out her few cosmetics and her utilitarian nylon brush and steel comb among these well-kept treasures. It was like an act of vandalism. That Joyce had decided to alter these long preserved arrangements by putting a portable television on a round table in one corner of the room was clearly the height of hospitality. She was making an all out effort, but almost certainly for John rather than for her unwanted guest.

Maya gave herself a light smack on the cheek. "Don't be unkind," she said, frowning at her reflection in the central glass of the mirror and carefully avoiding a disturbing view of herself in triplicate. "You have always wanted a real English life and here you have an authentic if outdated setting. In fact it might have been preserved just for you." She leant in closer and said slowly and firmly, as if instructing a naughty child, "You have your own chance to do something positive for John, an opportunity to get on genuinely friendly terms with Joyce. Do it!"

Later, in her adjoining room, Joyce gave herself similar instructions about using this time to build a better understanding with her daughter-in-law. Unlike Maya, she did not pause for long in front of the mirror. She was not without humour and did not lack self-awareness. "You haven't done very well so far. You can't look yourself in the eye, girl," she said aloud to her fleeting image.

Before meeting Maya, she had been worried about the fact that John, who had seen many of his local, boyhood girlfriends get married over recent years, had never brought any new ones home. She was unrepentantly old-fashioned and her life had been restricted to one of the more slowly changing corners of the modern world, but she was well aware of how things worked in that world and had always felt sure that he would not be living a solitary or celibate life in Cambridge. She had not allowed her mind to dwell on the details of this. Troubled by a nagging worry that it was his commitment to her and her welfare that stopped him from starting any serious relationship, she should have been relieved when he had told her about Maya and started bringing her with him every Sunday. It was not relief she had felt, however, but dismay. To her shame, she had realised that any worries she had about this girl stemmed from prejudice, a prejudice so deep-rooted that, until challenged by events, she had been totally unaware of it. It had been like an organic growth inside her. She half suspected that there was something like it deep within most people, on whichever side of the many human divisions they fell, no matter what group they belonged to or how enlightened they believed themselves to be, but that didn't excuse her. Her aim was John's happiness and she had set about overcoming not only a normal, if generally unacknowledged, sadness at losing her place as the most important woman in her son's life, but also this more sharply defined reluctance to accept, in that place, someone so other, so unexpected. With reserve on both sides, it was proving to be a slow process. Weekly meetings, initially polite but undeniably chilly, had become less so through sheer habit, but had not genuinely brought them any closer. It had taken a renewed frankness on John's part to make any real change likely. During their walk, after a long silence, he had confided in her as he had when a boy. "I know that you are finding things difficult with Maya, Mum, but if you only knew what she has been through you couldn't stop yourself from reaching out to her." Joyce had been shocked by what he had told her about London and Maya's total repudiation of her mother, but even more horrified by his description of her experiences with her parents and the extent to which she had been scarred by them. The picture he had painted, so vivid in his own mind that he had made totally real for her the figure of that frightened child on the landing battered by her parents' angry voices, had touched and moved her. Though she did not overestimate the seriousness of Maya's current condition, she was sorry to think of her having undergone yet more unhappiness.

Here they were, two women strangely and unexpectedly related, brought together from very different worlds by their shared love of one man, both with successes and hardships behind them and both with many of the same joys and sorrows ahead of them. Their origins and backgrounds did not alter such basic facts. Maya, even if she did not yet realise it, was someone who needed her. Joyce fell asleep with a surprised awareness that she was looking forward to the following day.

Maya was roused from a long dreamless sleep by the steady, hypnotic drone of a tractor working somewhere in the distance and the hysteric proclamation of a cock crowing close by. Usually she woke to the gentle sounds of John's presence, the reassurance she had come to depend on to give her a reason to move out into a new day. It took her a few bewildered moments to surface from a deeper sleep than she had known for a long time and make sense of these unfamiliar noises. Then she did hear someone moving about downstairs and could smell coffee and bacon but realised, with a small jolt, that today it was Joyce preparing breakfast.

The room was filled with a pale light and, as she got out of bed and drew back the curtains, she saw that yesterday's drizzle and gloom had gone and that the sun was breaking through a faint mist over the fields that stretched out beyond the back garden. Opening the window, she breathed in a cool, plant-scented breeze and was suddenly wide awake. All the lethargy and weakness of recent days vanished and she was eager to get outside into such a hopeful morning.

NINE

Arriving back in Cambridge, John rustled up a plate of sandwiches and a glass of beer and was just sitting down to a quiet evening of television when the phone rang. He leapt up to answer it, thinking it might be Maya calling. He was more on edge about her than he had supposed and sat down again, somewhat limply, the handset held slightly away from him, as he heard an unexpectedly deep voice on the line.

"John? It's Peter Fielding here. Sorry to interrupt your Sunday evening but I have been trying to get you all day and I thought it would be more difficult during a working week."

"Peter! Is something the matter? It's unusual to hear from you."

"Yes. Well. I had thought it is best for Maya if we kept out of your life for a while and left her to it. That seemed to me to be the only thing that we could do for her at present. However, as usual, Soshan isn't playing by the rules. I have just heard what she has been up to from a mutual friend with whom she is doing business. Apparently she was recently in London and met you both there. I'd like to speak to Maya. I think that, in the circumstances, I should meet her too."

John felt a hot spurt of anger. What was this, a game, a competition? He took a deep breath and told himself that adding his fury and frustration to an already unholy mix was not going to get them anywhere. He at least must stay cool and rational.

"Are you still there?" Peter sounded impatient.

"I'm sorry! I was thinking. Maya isn't here. I'm afraid that she has had a miscarriage. We should have let you know about it but it's all been rather hectic, though not too serious medically speaking. It happened at a very early stage and we hadn't even realised that she was pregnant. I'm not quite sure yet how she is taking it and I am a little concerned about her. I've just got back from taking her to Norfolk, for a week with my mother. I want her to have a complete break from everything. I'll be going again on Friday evening and will bring her back with me on Sunday. It might be best if you called her while I am there with her. I'll give you the number."

"I can imagine the kind of thing that you have been told about our family dynamic but I think I must insist on seeing Maya, especially after your news."

John had to suppress another flush of anger at this imperious tone but it was important to think things through. Maya had reacted violently, almost superstitiously, to the idea of having her parents in their home, so perhaps if her father persisted in this demand, there would be some merit in dealing with him on neutral territory. Not immediately though. She needed more time and he would have to talk to his mother before throwing *her* into the middle of all this.

"Look Peter, I'll be frank. I don't think you should contact Maya right now. It might be an idea, though, for you to see her in Hadleigh rather than Cambridge. Leave things for this week and this weekend. We will spend the following weekend there and you could come for the day on the Saturday. That gives Maya two weeks to recover and I can get in touch with my mother and make sure it's alright with her. I'll call you."

"Well, I don't want to be unreasonable. It would be good to see your village and, if at all possible, the farm that you told me about. Your grandfather's wasn't it and now your uncle's? Let's agree on that Saturday. By the way, I'll bring someone with me. She's a friend that I'd like Maya to know. We won't be any trouble. We'll stay in Norwich. We can come over at a time convenient for your mother. I'll await your call."

That was the end of the conversation. There was no chance to reply. Peter had achieved what he wanted and, wasting no further time, had put the phone down. He left John fuming. It was of little interest to him what Peter did with his life as long as he did nothing more to distress Maya. Bringing an unknown woman into her life without preamble or excuse might well do so. Did he care at all about how she might feel?

He returned half-heartedly to his sandwiches. He had lost his appetite. If Peter could rattle him so badly with one phone call, no wonder that he managed to infuriate Maya. This fraught situation, however, could not simply be written off or muddled through. Eventually it had to be resolved one way or another. Maya had a choice. She could either come to terms with her unsatisfactory parents or she could repudiate them with no regrets and no backward looks. He did not see the latter as an ideal, or even workable, solution. He had very little sympathy for Peter but recalling Soshan's bright, undaunted figure, he decided that her implicit appeal to him for help was not something that he could easily ignore. He wanted Maya to find a way back to her mother. He also had a more personal motive for such an outcome. The possibility of starting a family had been unexpectedly forced into his mind and if he eventually did have children, he would like them to know their grandparents on both sides, with no sad histories to complicate their lives. That sorry saga should end here. Even the worst parents can often make a better job of grand-parenting and that might be a final answer to all this.

As he went into his office building the next morning, he was surrounded by a group of Maya's colleagues. "How is Maya? Could you give us the address where she is staying? We'd like to send her a card straight away. We've got a small present for her if you could give it to her when you see her. Tell her we miss her."

He was pleased that Maya had made her mark here. She sometimes seemed so solitary, so dependent on him for companionship. He still spent occasional Saturday evenings with a group of male friends but these get-togethers had gradually become more infrequent and he thought this growing isolation from old companions was probably unhealthy. The men and girls here might offer only casual friendship but the thought that Maya had the possibility of any independent life beyond the one she shared with him was encouraging and lifted his gloomy mood.

While John was drawing comfort from these small things, Maya and his mother were well on the way to giving him more solid reasons to be cheerful. Living continuously together rather than passing an allotted, therefore rather artificial, period in each other's company, changed the rules of engagement. Necessarily involved in normal, daily routines and essential tasks, they became less self-conscious, behaved more naturally and each, without even meaning to, revealed more about herself to the other than ever before. They had both resolved to do better but found themselves doing so by force of circumstance rather than through any positive virtue or effort.

Another burst of glorious weather, holding out from day to day with no English meteorological tantrums or tears to break it up, also helped. Under blue skies and with the sun casting dappled shade through large trees onto the wide lawn, the garden was a delightful place. There, every day after breakfast and a cursory whip through household chores, Joyce gardened and Maya sat watching her. Slowly, she was drawn into helping out and into an unexpected pleasure.

"I was never really allowed to be dirty when I was a child." She glanced up at Joyce from the trough of compost where she had been put to planting out some seedlings. "This paddling my fingers in soil is probably something I should have done when young. It's wonderfully satisfying and soothing isn't it?"

Joyce held up her own grimy hands. "Getting stuck into the soil is a way of life for me. As a young man my father did hard labour on the land. By the time Robert and I were born he had raised himself well beyond that but he still insisted that we worked, really worked, in the fields and in the yard. He didn't want us to feel that we could just ride on the back of what he had achieved. And, yes, it is satisfying. I was often cross when he drove us as he did but I owe a lot to him. He left me with a good basis for a contented life."

"Joyce...." Maya hesitated, "there is something I have to say. I know I have disrupted your life and disturbed your contentment. I was a shock to you, wasn't I? Not the girl you wanted for John. I can see that you must have been lonely without him. You must have hoped he would marry the sort of girl you had always known, someone it would have been easier to share him with."

Joyce turned back to her planting and worked doggedly for several minutes without answering. Then she sat back on her heels, put down her trowel and wriggled her shoulders as if to ease a catch. "I would have carried on as usual after Fred died, that's how I was brought up to be, but without John there, still needing me, my heart wouldn't have been in it. So, yes, it was hard when he left home. He's exceptionally conscientious but he's also a normal young man and, to be honest, was already living a life of his own before he met you. Something every mother has to come to terms with. For me, without Fred, it was worse. The house sometimes feels so empty. There is no-one to share the small happenings of the day with, no-one to chat to about trivialities. I can't count on someone being interested in all my doings. Of course I was going to be envious of the person who shares all that with my son. I would have felt the same about anyone John married but...." She forced herself to look at Maya and took a deep breath. "It's difficult to admit this...." She paused again and then said, "Pretending things aren't as they are, is not going to help. Yes, I did find it harder because you seemed so different."

"Not just different," Maya sounded sad, "foreign. But I'm not what I seem. It's very frustrating to look like one thing on the outside and be something quite different on the inside. I have wasted a lot of energy raging against how unfair that is."

They both sat in silence. The sun shone, the birds sang and the trees sighed gently. It was incredible that misery and dissension were even possible in such a place.

"I want to be honest about something else." Joyce made an unusual and unexpected gesture, reaching out to grasp Maya's hand. She sat for a moment looking down at their muddy, intertwined fingers. "I've been talking to John, talking about you. He's told me more than you probably realise. I don't think he meant to or wanted to. It just happened. He needed some outlet you see. He was very worried about you. I'm sorry that things are at such a pass with your mother. I can partially understand what that must be like. I've never really got along with my own. We aren't even close enough to fight. We are just distant." She took Maya's other hand but looked away from her and into the garden. "This latest crisis....well, at times like this it would be good to have a mother. You are after all facing a loss. You need someone. John is very good but another woman.... that might help."

Maya's voice was low. "It doesn't feel like a loss; more like a functional failure. I didn't know.... I didn't expect.... I had never thought about children and I'm finding it hard to picture an actual baby." Her voice became so soft that Joyce had to turn back to her and lean closer to hear her. "It's a terrible thing to say but I think it was a relief. I know what harm can be done to a child. I'm still an emotional mess. I need more time. I'm not ready for motherhood. I don't know if I'll ever be ready."

Joyce said strongly, "Of course you will be. My mother never set me much of an example but I always knew I could do better than she did." She slowly shook her head and her face darkened. "For a while, I thought I'd never get that chance. That's something else about what has happened to you. It is bringing back memories of a terrible loss of my own." Her fingers tightened around Maya's. "I should have had a daughter. But, like you, I had a miscarriage. It was at a much later stage than yours. I had been so thrilled and happy. I had everything ready and waiting, a cot, a pram, heaps of pretty clothes. Afterwards, I just bundled everything up and sent it off to charity. I just wanted to get it all as far away from me as possible. Never see any of it again. I never talked about it. Talking wasn't going to help. Anyway, that was the way things were at that time. I'm sure it was bad for us. No way to cope with things. Both Fred and I silently struggled to get over it. When John was born it seemed that we had, but it has never really gone away. After Fred died, it was more than ever just my lonely secret." Her voice broke a little. "I won't pretend that there are easy answers to the things life throws at us. Happy endings aren't as common as we'd like but perhaps...." her voice again faltered, "perhaps we might see this as another chance. Maybe we could try to give each other a little of what we have both missed out on."

Suddenly, as if stung, she dropped Maya's hands, stood up and said harshly, "I don't know what's come over me. I should know better than to indulge in such idle talk. You are still convalescing. You should not be asked to think of anything beyond getting well. Take no notice of me. I'll go and get the recommended answer to all life's problems, a cup of tea."

Without waiting for any response, she strode back into the house and an extraordinary rattling of cups and spoons

91

gave an indication of just how unlike herself she was. On their recent tour of the farm, she had shown a fleeting readiness to open up, before taking fright and closing down. Today, she had not so much opened up as flung every barrier aside.

Maya, moved and even tearful, her own reticence and reluctance swept away, knew that she would have to tread carefully. It would be best to let Joyce set the pace. This could mean progressing in slow, small steps or, possibly, in intermittent, giant leaps but at last it was happening. They were coming closer. Life looked better than it had even a few hours ago.

When Joyce returned with the tea tray, she found Maya, her face composed, taking a conspicuous interest in the birds around her and looking up into one of the trees. "Can you hear that bird? I saw it briefly. It's such a pretty thing. Do you know what it is?"

"It sounds like a goldfinch." Joyce put the tray on a garden table. She looked hot and a little harried and clearly welcomed this diversionary tactic.

Sipping their tea, they talked a little self-consciously about birds and gardening and just as Joyce let out a puff of breath as if about to go back to where they had left off, the phone rang.

"That was John." She came back from the house with an odd expression. "He said not to bring you to the phone. He'll call again this evening when there's time for a long chat. Your father wants to see you and also, apparently, this village and the farm if it's possible. John is sounding us out about the idea of him coming to see you here. Not this week. Next weekend. He wanted us to talk it over before he rings later."

"This is because I've seen my mother." Maya sounded weary. "My dear father doesn't want her to have one over on him." Her tone hardened. "As to his interest in the farm, that won't be a desire to learn about rural England, it will be him looking to audit John's financial status. Well, John knows that I don't want either of them in our house. That's why he's asking you to be hostess. How do you feel about it? I hate to embroil you in all the horrors of the Fielding family just as we were.... well, you know....but it would certainly be less stressful for me."

"That settles it," Joyce said decidedly. "We certainly don't want things to be stressful for you. He can come here."

Exhausted by so much talking and a little alarmed by her own lack of reticence, she dropped heavily into a chair and, pointing to the teapot, mimed pouring, as if offering a reward, a celebration of all that they had achieved. They drank more, probably superfluous but nevertheless sustaining, tea in companionable silence, lost in thoughts of past difficulties and future possibilities. Maya was anxious to speak to John. He needed to tell his mother even more about her parents and make sure that she knew what she taking on in agreeing to allow her home to be invaded by Peter's potentially trying and disruptive presence.

TEN

Peter descended on Hadleigh in some style. He drove up just before midday, in a red, soft-topped BMW sports car from which he emerged looking like a male model in a glossy fashion magazine. He stood there surveying his surroundings and Joyce, coming out to greet him, was quite dazzled by his splendour. She had been left with only a vague impression of him after the Registry Office ceremony in December. All her attention had been concentrated on getting through the day without revealing any of her inner dismay and perhaps the gloomy winter weather had not done him justice. Now, with the sun glinting on his thick, blonde hair, dressed in impeccable chinos and a pale polo-necked sweater, he was revealed as a very handsome and impressive man, the faint lines around his eyes and the dusting of silver at his temples only adding to his air of distinction.

Maya now followed John through the front door and stood beside him on the step. "More like a visitation than a visit." Her whispered comment caused John to give her a swift, appraising look. He had already noticed that her manner towards his mother was considerably warmer and that she was looking much happier and more confident but, with the memory of her extreme reaction to her mother still potent, he had been nervous about how she would behave today and her robust response to Peter astonished and relieved him.

At that moment the passenger door of the car opened and two slim, tanned legs slid out. A small, dark-haired woman in a denim skirt and off-the-shoulder floral blouse, a cashmere sweater tied round her waist, unfolded herself from her low seat and stood beside the car, a fixed smile on her face.

"Joyce, I hope you didn't mind my bringing a friend." Peter beckoned to his passenger. "This is Karen. Karen, Joyce."

As the two women nodded to each other, about to speak, he put his hand on Karen's back and propelled her towards the house, leaving Joyce standing there, a little stunned.

"Good morning, John. Maya, you're looking surprisingly well given what I was told about you. Karen, meet my son-in-law and my rebel daughter."

"Hello Karen. Rebel is a bit harsh. Try to think of me as a freedom fighter. Sadly our family is best described in these military terms. Welcome to the war zone." Maya smiled sweetly at Karen who, if not exactly left with her mouth open, was certainly startled. Peter, his face thunderous, moved towards Maya, and she took a hasty step backwards.

"Peter, Karen, it's good to see you both." John rushed into speech, giving Maya a cold, repressive glare. "We are lucky it's such good weather because Mother has planned a buffet lunch in the back garden. Later, as Peter was keen to see my uncle's farm, we will go there for tea. Around three thirty or so. Right now, we'll get ourselves some drinks from indoors and take them out with us." He turned to Joyce who had still not moved. "You lead the way, Mum."

Peter, with a visible effort, controlled his temper and taking Karen's arm drew her aside to let Joyce pass. They followed her indoors as John held Maya back for a moment, his face and tone tight and angry.

"What are you thinking of. How can you be so thoughtless? I don't care how you feel about your father. Don't make things uncomfortable for Mum."

"Sorry. Sorry. He is just so arrogant, he makes me furious. And who is this woman? Why has he brought her along? No, it doesn't matter. You're right. Joyce is doing us a huge favour and I will behave."

They went out with their drinks to a group of chairs already arranged under the trees on the lawn and this peaceful setting worked a kind of magic. With the growing heat tempered to a pleasant warmth by the shade, the leaves stirred by a soft breeze, anger seemed inappropriate and harsh words almost unthinkable. On the pretext of wanting to see more of the garden, Peter, never still for long, soon drew John away for a private talk. They strolled off, holding their glasses and Maya, chatting to Karen and Joyce, was painfully alert to the muted sound of their conversation. When they returned, John gave her a small, encouraging wink and she had the impression that he had answered her father's important, practical questions and that all that was left for her to do was to answer the impossible ones about her state of mind. As Peter sat down next to her, his first words seemed to confirm this.

"John has told me about your job. Do you plan to carry on working, even if you decide to have children? Something that now appears to be a possibility. You may not have had a blazing academic record but you are a clever girl. Is this the kind of work that you want to do?"

"I enjoy it. It's reliable, secure, predictable." Every word was a gunshot and, chin raised, aimed at him like a weapon, Maya's face was flinty and challenging. She turned pointedly to Karen on her other side. "What do you do?"

"I'm the main receptionist at a private spa. It's small but very luxurious. Peter uses it. It's where we met."

"Fascinating!" Maya gave Peter a look, her eyebrows raised.

"Lunch is ready." John once again hastily intervened and, ushering them all onto the terrace, seated them at a long table shaded by a large umbrella. There was a selection of cold foods set out at one end of this and, for a while, there was something of a bustle as they selected what they wanted to eat, but slowly a combination of food, wine and sun induced a sleepy languor and conversation became more desultory and lost any sharp-tongued edge.

Maya, rousing herself to take trouble with Karen as a penance for having made her uncomfortable, discovered that her main interests appeared to be fashion, foreign holidays and Peter; probably in that order.

"It's lovely here," Karen looked round the garden, "but the weather in England is always so unreliable isn't it. Sunshine is my thing. For our last holiday we stayed in a wonderful hotel in the south of France. I adore the heat. I got a fabulous tan. I lived in a bikini for the whole fortnight, though I bought some fantastic clothes. The shops were incredible. Shopping is very much my thing. The food was absolutely wonderful. I had to be really strict with myself. It would have been easy to get positively fat. Not my thing. I need to look good for my job."

Karen's complacent smile suggested that she had little doubt about her looks. It was not quite clear who had been on this holiday with her. Had it been Peter? Maya decided to ask no questions. In any case, Karen, once launched on her favourite topics, really needed no more than an admiring audience and a gentle assenting murmur now and again was more than enough. Joyce, sitting beside them, nodded a lot and kept up a facade of interest, but in the end, she and Maya simply sat enjoying the sunshine and the garden, hardly disturbed by Karen's high-pitched, nasal voice and the underlying bass line of the men.

It was quite an effort to rouse themselves for the trip to the farm. Looking at Peter's polished leather loafers and the high heeled and precarious-looking sandals that Karen was wearing, John decided that they should drive there. He took Maya and his mother in his car and Peter and Karen followed in theirs.

Things got off to a good start. Robert, waiting for them in the porch, was impressed by the BMW and Peter by the size and appearance of the farmhouse. They had instantly summed each other up with an identical, calculating awareness and Peter, so smartly urban, Robert, so tweedily rural, recognised a kinship of purpose and outlook that outweighed superficial differences. Immediately engrossed in a businesslike conversation, they went inside together, leaving the others to follow, Karen teetering along in the rear. Robert stopped at the office door and turned to Joyce.

"Perhaps you three would like to wait in the sitting-room while John and I show Mr Fielding round, Joyce. I'm afraid you won't find Mother in her usual chair. She's in bed. She had a bit of a fall this morning. No broken bones, not even many bruises but it's shaken her and left her a bit confused. I'm sure that you'll want to go up and see her but it's probably better not to worry her with any other visitors. She's definitely not herself right now."

Joyce had already decided that it was necessary for her and Maya to stay inside with Karen, who was patently ill-equipped for any kind of walking and, though she pursed her lips at this directive, nodded her head curtly. The men then started off on their tour of the farm and she went up to see her mother, leaving Maya to continue coping with their unwanted guest.

Unwanted maybe, but despite her initial antagonism, Maya had by now almost begun to feel sorry for Karen and when, on the men's return, they were taken to the dining room to face one of Mrs Hemsby's huge teas while still digesting Joyce's substantial lunch, she felt that the poor woman was really suffering. Peter, who was deep in a discussion with Robert and John of the complicated bureaucratic and financial aspects of keeping the farm going, hardly took any notice of her. Obviously she had to pay a price for whatever she gained from her relationship with him.

When at last, the two of them, declining an invitation to return to Joyce's house, drove off into the summer evening, there were mixed impressions and emotions in the group standing outside to wave them off. Robert had a far more positive view of his nephew's wife, her English credentials now firmly established. Joyce, exhausted by both physical and social efforts and a difficult half hour with her mother, who had been worryingly frail, was thankful that the day was almost over. John was torn between annoyance with Maya for exposing his mother to possible embarrassment, a surprised admiration for the spirit she had shown in dealing with Peter and gratitude for her unexpected patience with

Karen. Maya, aware that she had not only faced up to but had also faced down her father, could not decide exactly how his new friendship, which she did not want to think of in any other terms or rate any higher, made her feel or whether it posed any kind of threat to her growing self-confidence and still fragile serenity.

They were glad that they had driven to the farm and did not to have to walk back to the cottage. They had left behind a lot of washing up and tidying up to be done there. Ignoring her protests and asking for the loan of nightclothes and toiletries, John and Maya insisted on staying overnight to help Joyce with it all and driving straight to work the next morning.

Stretching out tiredly in bed, watching John setting out things ready for this early start, Maya suddenly thumped her pillow. "What on earth does my father think he is doing? What can he possibly see in that woman? She's quite attractive I suppose, in her way, but I can't see what else she has to offer. An ego boost? How old do you suppose she is? Under thirty, would you say? Does he have to inflict her on us? He's ready enough to want me to find more demanding work. Look at what she does. A spa! Imagine him going to such a place. Does he have to fraternise with the staff, though?"

"Maya, do you know how snobbish and impossible that sounds? Leave it. You dealt admirably, if rather ferociously, with your father. I think you are going to find meeting him from time to time more manageable than I had feared." John got into bed and put his arms round her. "As for using spas, or seeing Karen, he is at that midlife stage after all and he must sometimes be very lonely." He turned off the lamp and drew her closer. "Forget him. Let's just think about ourselves. You can concentrate on me for a while."

Later, lifting her head from John's chest, Maya said sleepily, "If only we could stay here like this forever."

As he turned slowly onto his side without answering, she refitted herself more comfortably into the curve of his body and murmured, "Right now everything seems so simple. I don't want to ever get up and face all those dreadful people who make everything so messy and complicated." Her eyes closed and her voice tailed off, "My father....so stupid....a woman like that....after my mother....it's a travesty."

There was no response. John was already asleep.

ELEVEN

The rented house outside Cambridge might be their first shared home but they were not sentimental about this. It was a stopover, somewhere to sleep and eat between working days. John had chosen it because it offered a travelled space, a defining distance, to separate them from work but was not too distant, and though small and easy to maintain, it was not so small as to be cramped or uncomfortable. It was a shelter. It served his present needs but his past, his future and his heart were anchored in Hadleigh. For Maya, any physical surroundings were, for now anyway, irrelevant. Home was wherever John happened to be.

Yet, returning to it that Monday evening, they came indoors with a compelling sense of homecoming. Having driven straight to the office from Norfolk that morning, they were very tired and being among the familiar, chosen arrangement of their own belongings, free from any compulsion to consider the needs of other people, was extraordinarily potent.

All that they wanted to do was freshen up and have an early meal but as Maya was starting to prepare supper, the phone rang. Apprehensive of its potential as a source of trouble, she came to the kitchen door and stood there caught up in one side of a conversation between John and the caller.

"Soshan.".... "Ah, you got my message. I thought you ought to know what had happened." He looked guiltily over his shoulder at Maya who was glaring at him. "No, no, nothing like that"...."Really there is nothing to worry about and she is already fit again."...."She had a complete rest with my mother"...."So Peter's been in touch." He shot Maya a look, his eyes wide and placatory. "Lunch with my mother and tea at my uncle's farm."...."Yes, he was very impressed."...."No, he didn't really upset her"...."Actually, she was quite tough with him".... "Yes, she was more than tough on you."

Maya came over to him and held out her hand for the phone. He hesitated but she frowned and gestured impatiently and he reluctantly passed it to her.

"Hello. It's me. I didn't know that John had told you about what happened. It wasn't something to worry you about. I am over it. I'm fine." She said nothing for a while and then spoke loudly and forcefully, as if overriding a torrent of speech coming at her, "Listen, it was not a tragedy or a crisis but we have had a trying week or two and, yesterday, Dad's visit to contend with." She held the handset slightly away from her with an exasperated sigh, but returning it to her ear said firmly, "He was the same as always and no, I don't give him special treatment. I hardly see him these days. This get-together was his idea." She paused, then blurted out, "I'm sorry about *our* meeting in London. I realise that I behaved badly. I've been thinking things over and talking to John. He's made me see that we should keep in touch." Her face tightened and she made as if to end the call but, drawing in a deep breath, said harshly, "Just give me time. I'll write to you. I have to think carefully about what I want to say and for that a letter will be best. Now, I was just getting our supper so I'll pass you back to John."

She rushed off into the kitchen, closing the door firmly on the end of John's next sentence, "Soshan, I hope that has made you feel better. Let's try...."

Five minutes later, he came into the kitchen and stood looking at Maya who was violently chopping carrots. "I don't know who those poor vegetables are standing in for but I feel sorry for him or her. Is it safe to give you a hug?"

She gave a strangled laugh. "Sorry. We don't have to talk about Mother do we?"

"No." John came towards her, his arms out. "I'm glad that you said sorry and pleased that you said you'd write to her but, for now, we'll just get on with things and give it all a rest."

That week passed peacefully until the Friday, when the phone, which Maya was beginning to imagine as lurking in the hall, a messenger of disaster, rang just as they got home.

"John, I just wanted to warn you that things will be different this weekend." It was Joyce and she sounded flustered. "It's your grandmother. She's had a second fall and become even more confused and quite ill. We are keeping her in bed but with some difficulty. Robert isn't managing too well and I'm staying at the farm with them. It would help if he had you to talk to. He doesn't put much store by anything I say. It's as if he has aged overnight and I'm worried about him too. I'm sorry to put you out but I wondered if you could come tomorrow morning. You can sleep at the cottage and get some rest from him at night, but be at the farm in the day."

Iva, a small woman whose indomitable spirit had always given her added stature, now looked even smaller in her large bed, almost submerged in a feather mattress and large soft pillows. Her face was colourless and her bright eyes milky and hooded. Bending down to greet her, Maya breathed in a scent that reminded her of old newspapers and long-closed rooms. The lavender water that Joyce had sprayed around lavishly could not override the discomforting evidence of extreme age and the earthy realities of physical decay.

"Are you Joyce's girl?" Iva looked doubtfully up at Maya. "No. That didn't happen after all." Maya heard Joyce's sharp intake of breath. "Such a quiet one, Joyce. She didn't want to talk to me about all that, you know. Robert used to tell me everything. He could be moody but he was mostly a good boy. Not like his father though. No-one could ever match Nathan." Her eyes misted and her mouth trembled.

Joyce, who had come round to the other side of the bed, spoke loudly and firmly. "This is Maya, Mother, John's wife. John is talking to Robert and then he is coming up to see you."

"Is Nathan coming? I want to see Nathan. He'll sort things out for me. He always knows what to do." She lay for a few moments, seemingly unaware of them, then turned to Maya and said with startling clarity, "Make my grandson happy. He's a good boy. Don't worry about what anyone says or thinks about you. You are such a pretty girl, but remember that it's not looks that count. I wasn't ever pretty but I was what Nathan wanted." Her eyes closed, she again retreated into the unknown, breathing heavily, but as Joyce drew up a chair and sat down beside the bed, she found herself unexpectedly caught in a momentary flash of her mother's intense, blue gaze.

"Joyce, there you are. Always such a sensible girl. I never needed to watch out for you. And you found a good man.

Robert now, he was never going to find anyone. I always knew that. I never told Nathan what I knew. He wouldn't have understood. He was always puzzled by Robert's failure to find a wife. The only love Robert ever really felt was for the farm. I had to watch out for your brother. I'm sorry. I thought you could manage, you see." She held out a trembling, freckled hand and said softly, "It's good to have you here. Give me a kiss."

A fleeting look of total shock passed over Joyce's face. Then her mouth twisted and she sat awkwardly upright, not meeting Iva's eyes or responding in any way. She was visibly relieved to see John come into the room.

"Gran, how are you?" He came over and gently touched Iva's soft, wrinkled cheek but she was half asleep once more and taking in his mother's expression, he went round to her and gave her a hug. "Go and talk to Robert, Mum. I'll stay here for a while and give you a much needed break."

"No! No, I can't handle Robert right now. I can't."

"It's alright, Joyce. Stay here with John. I'll go down and sit with Robert." Maya gave John a reassuring look and went downstairs.

In the sitting room, Robert was hunched in his chair. She was shaken to see how frail and unkempt he looked. She had not seen him often, but he had always appeared so upright, so spruce, so well-groomed. She moved towards Iva's customary seat opposite him but could not quite bring herself to sit there and coming back, pulled over a stool and sat close beside him.

"John is staying upstairs with your mother for a while. She wants to be there, so I've come to keep you company. Can I get you anything?"

Robert made an effort to sit straighter and tried, ineffectually, to tidy his hair which had become rather dishevelled. "Oh, Maya, I'm sorry. I'm not quite myself at the moment. Mrs Hemsby was here for a while and she brought me a cup of tea. I don't need anything, thank you." He looked anxiously at her, "How was Mother?"

"Well, I don't think she is in pain but she isn't herself and when she speaks, keeps moving between the past and the present."

"She is going isn't she? She won't get over this. I just don't know what I shall do." For a few moments he stared into the fireplace, his face bleak. Then he shook his head and said defensively, "It must seem pathetic to you. An old man who can't see how he'll manage without his mother." He gave her a sidelong look. "She's always been here, you see. I don't have.... I've never had anyone else. My father was always a bit frightening but she was there to smooth things over for me. Even as she got old she never lost her spirit, never gave in to age and I had got used to feeling that she'd always be here. I still can't believe that she won't be."

Maya took his hand but, at his slight recoil, dropped it. "We hardly know each other yet but you have to try to see me as an extension of John. You trust and rely on him. I know that you have your doubts about me but I hope you will come to trust me too. We will both do all we can to help."

Robert nodded, an almost furtive smile touched his face but he said nothing and they sat in a strained silence, reserved strangers forced into an inescapable intimacy. The disintegration of a man she had seen managing this large farm so efficiently was very disconcerting.

She had always put her own inadequacies down to a lack of proper maternal care and, in this context, the definition of 'proper' had been decided by her. She had sulked and pouted like a child for years. Confronting a mirror image of such behaviour, she did not like what she saw. Here was someone cradled and cosseted all his life, given an excess of maternal attention without apparently gaining anything from it, his inadequacies now shamefully and publicly on display. She thought of Joyce, whose share of that attention had been unfairly diverted to this crumbling man but who, faced with loss upon loss and long, lonely years, had simply carried on and given her son just the right backing to make him the man he now was, without ever allowing a sense of grievance to stunt her. Her mother-in-law might be an obscure countrywoman but she was successful in all the important ways.

She was beginning to understand what these ways were. It wasn't John, however much he gave her by way of love and support, who would rescue her. Life was tougher than that. There was no rescuer, no rescue. She had to find in herself the necessary courage to overcome the past and prevent it from spoiling her future. She had already made some progress; gaining professional qualifications, finding a job unaided, then getting married. If she had compromised that new-found independence with her readiness to lean on John, she was at last, at least, learning what she was doing wrong. That was a start. Hopefully she was on her way to making a better job of her life.

Though Joyce was staying at the farm and spent a lot of time with her mother, she did not have much actual work to do. Nurses had been found. One came in the morning to wash Iva and give her breakfast and a second nurse came in the evening to prepare her for sleep and to sit with her through the night. Mrs Hemsby continued to come in daily to prepare food and carry out her usual chores. Yet Joyce was looking totally exhausted and when they all sat down to meals together, she barely ate anything. It was clearly emotional rather than physical stress that was wearing her down and as they were leaving on the Sunday evening, Maya said regretfully, "I wish we could stay but I can't take any more time off. We'll be back next Friday evening. We'll be with you about seven. Take care of yourself."

They heard nothing more that week but as they drew up outside the farm on Friday, Joyce came out to meet them, her face pale.

"It's over. She's gone. It happened about an hour ago. There was no chance to get in touch with you. I'm sorry to greet you with such news. One of the nurses is in the sitting room with Robert. He's in a bad way. Can you go and see him, John?"

John went over and drew her to him but she gently loosened herself from his grasp. "I'm alright. I think your uncle really urgently needs you. Maya, we should leave him to John and the nurse. We'll go into the kitchen and have a drink. I find it the most comforting place at the moment. I'm really cold. I'm shivering, in fact, and the Aga makes it warm. We'll have our supper there. Mrs Hemsby has put something ready for us in the oven. Robert may have to be put to bed. He may not want, may not be able, to eat." She seemed oddly compelled to talk. "Anyway the doctor is coming. He said he'd be here as soon as he can." For a second her voice wavered. "He has to do the official things that are necessary and he will look at Robert too."

In the kitchen, Maya made her sit down, poured a small brandy and put it into her unresisting hand. "I think something stronger than tea for you this time. I'm too tired for alcohol. I'll have a juice." She was hoping that such banalities might take the blind look off Joyce's face and bring her back to something more like herself. She did take an absent-minded sip of her drink but she choked on it and Maya had to take the glass from her.

"Maya, you were there the other day. You saw what happened. Mother asked me to give her a kiss. After all these years! I just couldn't do it. You won't believe it, but there have been times when I've kissed utter strangers simply because I was trying not to look old-fashioned or standoffish. With Mother I couldn't even make that kind of empty gesture. My whole body revolted against it. I didn't want, I couldn't bring myself, to touch her." Her face looked grey with exhaustion. "Whatever she had done, whatever bitterness I felt, that was wrong. And now there is no chance to make things right. It's all over. I thought I'd never forgive her but I'm left wondering if I'll ever forgive myself."

This outburst was almost too much for Maya. It was all too close to home for her to dare any response. She turned with relief as John came in. He went over to his mother and, his voice dark with worry, told her that the doctor had arrived.

"I'll go up with him to Gran's room." He hesitated and then said gently, "They will take her away this evening. You might find that difficult and want her to stay here. It is a bit sudden and brutal I know, but it will be for the best. The doctor will arrange everything. You don't need to do anything. Afterwards he'll look Robert over. Then I want him to look at you, Mum. You are very pale and with all that has to be done you need to keep well."

The evening ended with Robert in bed under heavy sedation. There had been so much to do that they had forgotten to notify Iva's night nurse that she would not be needed so, when she came in as usual, she simply took up her place in his room. Joyce, who had submitted to John and stayed in the kitchen while the undertakers carried Iva downstairs, but had insisted on standing at the front door and watching them drive away, was shivering again and was also sent to bed with a mild sleeping pill. All this dealt with, John and Maya, deciding that it was best for them to stay at the farm and be on hand in case of any further crises, rummaged around, finding sheets and pillowcases in a linen cupboard and making up what had been a long unused bed in the guest bedroom.

John had worked all day, driven from Cambridge and spent a difficult evening dealing with the undertakers and the doctor, arranging for the care of his uncle and trying to make things easy for his mother. The strain of it all together with his own genuine, if muted, grief had exhausted him. The room was cool and dark, the moonlit world beyond the heavy curtains totally silent and he fell instantly into a deep sleep.

Maya could not sleep for a long time. She had never experienced a death before. She could not grieve for Iva, someone she had hardly known, but she could not shake off thoughts of the finality of what had happened, the cold realisation of all animation, all feeling ending in this blank nothingness, of a vital personality becoming an object that had to be disposed of. She stared into the darkness of the room. Did anything survive of that intense character Iva had been?

At that moment, the long silence was broken by the eerie hooting of an owl drifting up from the meadow beyond the walled garden. It was a haunting, even frightening, sound at such a moment. Maya knew that she was being childish and, worse than that, was trivialising the awesome experience of death, but banal, conventional images of ghosts flashed through the night and were difficult to suppress. She snuggled closer to John and tried to put any morbid thoughts out of her mind. Soothed by his warmth and nearness, she too slept.

TWELVE

A faint light was filtering through the heavy curtains into Maya's half opened eyes. She was drowsily aware of the solidity of John's body and still lulled by the rhythm of his deep, even breathing. Normally, he was up before she woke but he was still sleeping soundly and this, together with the unfamiliar surroundings, left her disorientated. She opened her eyes fully and looked cautiously round the shadowy room. Then, easing herself away from John and sliding out of bed, she collected her clothes and tiptoed across the landing into the bathroom. She gave her face a cursory rinse with cold water and hastily pulled on jeans and a T-shirt. She could have a proper wash later when there was no danger of disturbing anyone.

There was no sound. All the other bedroom doors were closed and, once downstairs, she saw by the clock in the kitchen that it was not quite six. Perhaps being in a strange bed had affected her. She had never been awake so early before.

With a guilty sense of intrusion, she walked almost stealthily through the house. It was still largely unknown territory. She had a clear picture of the individual rooms that she had been in but no mental map of the way that they fitted into the whole layout; no grasp of the building as a living entity. She was trying not to think about the fact that it might one day belong to John. This exploration, though irresistible in such uninhabited silence, was already making her uncomfortable enough. With Iva's death and the likely upheaval this would cause, it felt slightly indecent. Yet in spite of such scruples, she was led on by her fascination with the place and particularly by an unsatisfied curiosity about what lay beyond a small door on the sidewall of the dining room. She had noticed this during their meals there and the size of the door and its unlikely location had intrigued her and led her imagination, feeding on the age and atmosphere of the place, to run rather wild, though commonsense urged that it must be just a cupboard. Opening this door with some trepidation, she found a small room that was far more ordinary than any of her more unlikely fancies but still intriguing. It was clearly someone's much-loved sanctuary, Iva's most probably. A large bay window, set in the far wall, overlooked bushes and shrubs in a wilder part of the garden and under this window, beside an oval coffee table, was a high-backed, sagging armchair filled with tapestry cushions. There was a large, square pine table pushed up against one side-wall and on this stood an electric sewing machine and a miniature shelf unit that held stationery and assorted ceramic containers filled with pens and pencils. Below this work space were several baskets leaning against one another and overflowing with remnants of material, balls of wool, reels of cotton and skeins of embroidery silks, all spilling out into a colourful pool on the floor. The walls were hung with an array of framed photographs, many of them faded to a pale sepia. It was like a museum exhibit and it would take quite a time to examine all the faces on display.

Before she could even begin to do this, Maya started at the sound of someone else moving about beyond the dining room. Quietly closing the door on her interesting find and leaving any questions about it for later, she followed the sound back to the kitchen and saw the night nurse putting the kettle on.

"Oh! Good morning. Mrs Carter isn't it? You are up early. I'm just making tea. Would you like some?"

"Thank you. That would be welcome. How is your patient? I'm sorry but I don't know your name."

"I'm Nurse Watson. Mr Cole has slept all night and is still sleeping. The doctor said that he wasn't bearing up as well as he might be and gave him quite a strong sedative. Heartbreak isn't just a metaphor. It can be a real physical event. I hope that when he wakes he will have had time to recover."

As they sat looking at each other over the table, sipping their hot tea, Maya realised that the nurse was much older than her smooth, round face had at first suggested. This and the odd intimacy of their early morning solitude led her to voice troubling thoughts.

"I've never known anyone to die before. I hardly knew my husband's grandmother but I saw enough of her to realise that she was a very forceful presence and now there is nothing there anymore. I find that frightening. You get caught up in situations that seem as if they will go on forever. I keep thinking of the time and energy I spend on disagreements and disputes with people in my life. What if they were to die? I could be fighting shadows. That's also frightening. Don't you find it upsetting? Getting to know, getting involved with, others even if briefly, and then they are gone?"

"Well, when you first have to cope with someone's death it can be hard. It sounds heartless, but I soon learned to concentrate most of my attention on the practical tasks involved in caring for a patient. By focussing on those it becomes just a job. If it wasn't, I couldn't do it."

After a long silence, Maya said, "What is it like? Dying, I mean. Is it painful?"

When Nurse Watson put her cup down with a sharp sound she thought she had probably crossed a line and said more than was acceptable but, with a sort of resigned shrug, her companion answered quietly, " I wouldn't like to decide if it is painful or not. I won't talk about the horrific cases where pain is always and obviously there. Generally, it has looked to me as though those who take life as it comes take death in the same way and let go easily. People who have fought things in their lives, fought for and against things and taken life hard, fight with every last breath to hold on to it. That does look and sound painful and is distressing to see." She stood up. "I shouldn't be talking like this. I must go back to Mr Cole. Your husband has arranged for the doctor to call early this morning and he may need my help. I don't know if I shall be wanted here tonight so maybe I won't see you again. Take care of yourself. Don't be too upset. Mrs Cole had lived a long life. We all have to die. It doesn't help to dwell on it. All we can do in the meantime is get on with things." She took their cups to the sink and went out of the kitchen without saying anything more, leaving Maya somehow ashamed of having pushed her into an awkward situation.

To shake off her uncomfortable feelings, she went out into the tiled passage and sliding back a heavy bolt on the rear door, stepped out into the walled garden and a bright morning. Here, the dim hush of the house behind her, she stood listening to a jaunty chorus of birdsong coming up from beyond the wall. She walked over, opened the gate and looked across the meadow outside. Joyce, almost despite herself and her determinedly prosaic manner, had already imbued this with an aura of romance by describing it as the scene of her engagement and now, the trees at the far end of it still faintly blurred by the remnants of a morning mist, it had a suitably dreamlike appearance. Above and around the stream, gleaming silver wherever it emerged from the tall grasses, there was an intense flurry of purposeful activity. The birds were not only singing. They were busy. There was a continual whirring of wings as they went about the daily business of finding food and water.

Maya sat down on the step in front of the gate and watched them. All this energetic bustling about was an antidote to the silence and sorrow indoors, an escape from her fears and doubts but was also, in her rather introspective mood, a reminder that life and death are co-existent and that both can be difficult.

"There you are." John had come up behind her. He sat down and put an arm round her waist. "I've never woken up without you beside me before. It felt odd. What got you up and about so early?"

"I must have slept more soundly than usual. I was probably worn out. This is the first time that anyone I know has died and I've been thinking deep thoughts. It was very dark and quiet last night, too. The only sound I heard was sad and rather scary. I think it was an owl hooting. I know that the scary bit was my imagination at work and it's comforting to get real and watch all these other little birds, to see that life goes on."

"Maya, there is a possibility that life may go on very differently for us now. Have you ever thought about this place being your home some day?"

"Well, you told me that you would almost certainly take it over in the future but, until today, that was always too far ahead of us to think about. Are you saying that it might happen sooner than you expected?"

"I think it might well do. We will have to see how my uncle rallies. But it won't be easy for him to live in this big house alone and Mum won't want to move in with him. It might mean I have to step in. Come inside now and have some breakfast. We'll get through the next week or so and see how things go after the funeral."

A fortnight later, they waited with Robert and Joyce in the hall of the farm. Since no distant relatives had kept up any contact with either her or Nathan for many years, they were Iva's only immediate mourners and, in deference to her age and the customs she had lived by, were all dressed in formal black.

Hadleigh Church was such a short distance away that there had been a suggestion that the coffin could be carried there and that they could follow it on foot, making it a truly rural funeral. However, Robert, though he was putting on a brave show and standing erect and unaided, seemed to be holding up more through moral determination than physical strength. Walking would clearly be too much for him. So they drove slowly behind the hearse in a funeral car so large and opulent that it cruelly emphasised the smallness of their group. This was more than compensated for by the number of other mourners who had made their own way to the church and found it unable to hold such an unexpectedly large congregation. As the priest led their procession slowly along the churchyard path, it passed through a considerable crowd forced to remain outside. Formally dressed, their heads bowed, they were strangely shadowy in the bright sunshine. As the coffin entered the even more shadowy, dim interior, everyone inside rose and, greeted by this solemn rustle, the magnificence of the organ and the sonorous words of the priest, the family carefully and ceremoniously arranged themselves in the front pew left empty for them.

Maya had no religion and no experience of religious rites. Her father was an out and out materialist and though her mother was rooted in a community held intact and shaped by its ancient Zoroastrian faith, for her this had always been more a question of habits and customs than doctrine or belief and she had never overtly brought any of this into her English life. Maya knew very little about it.

A solid grounding in books and films, old and new had, however, made a recurrent scene – a group of people standing round a grave, dressed in black and listening to a priest – part of her mental landscape. This literary and cinematic set piece had also crept onto television screens, where it frequently featured in popular detective series. Constant repetition had almost reduced it to a cliché. Yet something about the power and poetry of the words spoken rescued it from such a fate. It was important to both believers and non-believers. Finding herself part of such an iconic ritual felt weirdly unreal and she wondered if this almost inescapable element of theatricality might, in fact, help to distance people from grief.

At the graveside, it did, at first, appear to be helping Robert who stood straight-backed and composed but as the priest spoke the final words of commitment, he faltered and almost fell. John, standing next to him, caught his arm and, followed by the others, led him slowly back towards the church. Leaning heavily on his nephew, Robert looked ashen and drew harsh, laboured breaths, but once they managed to reach the church door and were surrounded by the many people waiting to offer sympathy, he revived considerably. These were people that they had known for years and Maya, a little on the edge of it all, thought rather bitterly that, however solemn the occasion, many of them were taking a chance to give John's foreign-looking wife a discreet inspection. She was slightly ashamed of her inappropriate gratification that today, no matter what doubts they had about her, they were seeing her in a situation where she was indisputably one of the Home Farm family.

Mrs Hemsby, as one of the mourners, had been persuaded, with some difficulty, to turn over what she now regarded as her kitchen to outsiders. As soon as she arrived back from the church, however, she went at once to inspect the buffet laid out in the farm dining room by the caterers, her face tight and her lips thin.

"It's a bit of a show really," Joyce confided to Maya. "She wants to emphasise her position as queen of the kitchen to all her friends but she is genuinely upset about Mother. They've shared this house for so long. This little pantomime helps her to get through today."

The whole village seemed to have turned up and there were also many associates whom Robert knew through his various farming dealings and shooting syndicates and women whom Joyce met regularly at various groups in neighbouring villages. Looking round the crowded rooms, Maya could see how naturally and easily everyone mingled. It was almost possible to forget why they were all here. It was becoming more like a normal social gathering. What had begun with a hushed murmur slowly increased in volume to a muted roar and there was even the odd laugh, swiftly suppressed.

Though John kept returning from duty tours of the room to introduce her to old schoolmates and other friends from his childhood, she began to feel lonely and isolated. She was never actually alone, there was always someone coming up to speak to her but she was very conscious of the effort they were making. Her earlier confidence at appearing as one of the family was fading. She was an outsider still.

She had spent six months looking at life as the Maya and John story. There were minor characters involved – colleagues, a few social acquaintances, relations existing very much on the sidelines. Her parents were a shadowy threat to its 'happy ever after' ending, but a hard core within her had melted when she had come closer to Joyce in a way that she had convinced herself was impossible with her own mother and she had finally allowed her mother-in-law a role in it. Yet, today's revelation of just how much of John existed beyond their narrow boundary as a couple was hard to take. These were all people who had been an important part of his life for years before she had ever known him, people with whom she had no connection. If he decided that they must leave Cambridge and return here, they were people with whom she would have to share him, people who looked at her and saw someone that they could not immediately feel comfortable with.

At last, as if by agreement, it was over. There was a general exodus that threatened to go on endlessly with everyone wanting to shake hands with Robert and Joyce and a final huddle round John at the main door, where stragglers wanted a quiet word with him.

"Look after the old boy, John. He's taken a knock."

"Good to know that Robert has you to help him out, John."

"We'll hope to see more of you, John....and your wife."

Maya saw that Robert had now retreated to his fireside seat but she could not see Joyce anywhere and went looking for her. In the dining room, where the caterers were busily clearing away the remaining food, she noticed that the door of the inner room was slightly ajar and going into the room beyond found her sitting in the armchair under the window, holding one of the tapestry cushions, slow, silent tears running down her face.

"Oh, Joyce," she went and knelt beside her, "I wish I could help. I'm so green. How can I have any idea of what you must be going through? I'm so sorry."

"I'm not grieving over Mother's death. I think that I'm grieving for her life or rather our life together. This was her room you know. As children we weren't allowed in here – ever. Even Robert was kept out. I can't remember my father being in here either. She said it was a place where she wasn't Mrs Cole or Mother, she was simply Iva. She spent hours here sewing or embroidering. All these cushions were her handiwork. There are things all over the house that she made. I don't mind that I never knew this seamstress, this Iva she retreated into. I do mind that I never really knew her as Mother. No child sees the person inside a parent, or they didn't when I was young. Now as a matter of course, of pride even, we spill our inner selves onto the world. But probably children still don't want to know all that. Father or Mother is what they want, not a personality with a background and a biography. The only parental emotion they are interested in is the love they crave for themselves. That was something that I never felt I was given. I wasn't neglected. I was fed and watered, educated as far as was considered necessary, but that was it." She put down the cushion she was holding and wiped her face with her sleeve. "I must get myself together. Funerals do this to you. It's not just losing someone. It's all the ceremony. It sets off things inside you. Maya, I want to say one thing. I see all this with my mother as a failure. I don't know whose failure. I don't think it was mine – but failure anyway. I did reject her last, small offer of affection. That was harsh and death puts an end to any possibility of making things different or better. Try not to do anything that means you might end up feeling like this. Sort things out while you have the chance. If it doesn't work because other people don't do their bit, at least you will know that you tried."

She stood up and carefully rearranged all the cushions in the chair. "Come on. I'll need to see how Robert is and we all need to consider what we are going to do next." She led the way out into the dining room, and closed the small door firmly behind them.

THIRTEEN

It might never have aroused any special warmth in them but as they faced the possibility of leaving it, the Cambridge house, more than at any time since they had lived there, had become a welcoming and relaxing place. Still slightly raw from the fallout of Maya's inner turmoil and the worry of her miscarriage, with unresolved questions about how best to treat her parents, they were glad of a refuge from the added demands of other people but it was only a temporary and partial escape.

Robert had unexpectedly pulled himself back from the physical and emotional brink on which he had been teetering. The day after the funeral, he had surprised them all by appearing in his tweeds, pulling on his boots and going straight into his normal routine. There was something about the natural rhythms of working the land that offered a particular brand of healing and that, over the following days, in defiance of his continued unsteadiness, seemed to be holding him together and enabling him to carry on.

Everyone felt it unlikely that he would cope as well with leisure time and loneliness. It was summer, harvest was underway and farming days were long, but there were still solitary hours to pass before sleeping. It did not do to think of him facing the empty chair opposite him in the sitting room. He would need help and companionship. After much discussion a compromise was reached.

Joyce agreed to spend evenings and nights at the farm from Monday to Thursday while John and Maya would drive straight there from work every Friday and return to Cambridge early each Monday morning. During their weekend stay, Joyce would spend all her time back in her own cottage but join them for a Sunday lunch prepared by Mrs Hemsby. It was not an ideal arrangement for any of them but they were all prepared to give it a trial.

The next few weeks passed comparatively peacefully, though they were always tired. The evening journeys, the necessary forward planning and the sheer level of effort involved in constant relocation were wearing. Frequently missing an important paper or item of clothing lost or forgotten in the transfer could be irritating and frustrating. They were always rootling through their luggage for some necessity or other, while generally pretty much resigned to not finding it.

Yet life somehow settled down, not always entirely satisfactorily but predictably and even enjoyably. Mrs Hemsby, her reassuring presence bolstering Robert's brittle confidence, continued to do all that she had always done and it was a bonus to have meals provided and housework taken care of. Any chores in their own house were sadly neglected but they discovered ways to ease the strain of living in two places at once. They each kept a spare set of essential toiletries and a basic wardrobe in Hadleigh and this, literally lightening their load, meant that they only needed to think about packing a few, more or less inessential, extras. On arrival, they could run unencumbered up to what became known as their room and change into casual clothes without any need to hoist bags upstairs or unpack. Maya kept some of her books on her bedside table and John took to storing his journals and paperwork in a large briefcase that went with him everywhere as a matter of course, so that fewer papers were lost in transit.

Maya was aware of a growing affection for the house. She was not intimidated by its size. She had adjusted to living in small rooms in Cambridge but had always previously lived in large houses, even though her father's, if substantial and spacious, was boxy and suburban in comparison with this rambling place. She delighted in a regained expansiveness. The nooks and crannies and unexpected storerooms and attics she was discovering spoke of a more carefree approach to life and offered a more laid-back and less regimented existence.

She was discovering other pleasures. She had always been a city girl. She was used to a garden but, since her parents were also essentially city people, a garden that had been a restrained, orderly arrangement of well-behaved plants around large areas of gravel and paving. It was viewed as merely a framework for the house. It had never been a place in which to actually spend time. Here there was a whole breadth of green, untrammelled countryside laid out before her, much of it belonging to her new family and with the weather staying gloriously, unendingly warm and dry, there was a constant temptation to be outside in the sunshine.

Each morning, after an undisturbed and dreamless sleep in the quiet night, she woke early and went down to sit at her favourite spot in the gateway of the walled garden, looking out over the meadow. With the farm workers also up at first light during this busy season, she could usually hear the steady drone of a combine in a nearby field. She was lulled into an unaccustomed state of pure contentment. John, now knowing where to find her, would join her, bringing mugs of coffee, and they would sit there companionably for a while before going in to have breakfast with Robert when he returned from his morning round of the yard and fields. John knew a great deal about all the birds flying around so busily and she was learning to recognise them and know their names. One morning, they even had a rare, daytime sighting of the owl.

"Maya, quick, look. There's your ghost."

She followed John's pointing finger and saw the pale, graceful spread of the bird's wings as it glided silently above the grass and disappeared into the trees. Its sheer beauty strengthened her growing pleasure at hearing its night time cry. She no longer associated this with death and sorrow. She now found it soothing rather than eerie, listening out for it and a little sad when she did not hear it.

"Even if Gran is missing this place and haunting it," John had said, half laughing when he guessed how her mind had been working, "she would be a more silent presence. She is hardly one to wail and moan."

This down-to-earth humour at first shook Maya but she saw how it sprang from a robust approach to living and dying that was gradually drawing her in and resetting her default mode. Her long-ingrained wariness was giving way to a more positive readiness to think well of everyone and everything.

Robert, by nature taciturn and undemonstrative, said little about their new arrangements but was slowly beginning to accept her as part of his life. He was out of the house before she came downstairs in the mornings and it was recognised that he could not be expected to be sociable over breakfast or lunch which he saw as merely necessary refuelling operations, but he did make more of an effort over supper. It helped that he was busy all day and that it was late in the evening before they all gathered in the sitting room. There, because the two men spent most of the time going over the events of the working day and discussing plans for the next one, it seemed natural for John to take over his grandmother's chair while Maya retreated to a small recliner in a corner of the room. She was usually half immersed in a book, half aware of this prosaic background murmur, looking up from time to time in response to a question or remark from one or other of them. Gradually, the residual tensions carried over from her childhood eased and an unsatisfied longing for such quiet domesticity was assuaged.

Occasionally, on a Saturday, when John went off with Robert, either about the farm or to some meeting or gathering connected with it, she would walk along the village street to Joyce's house and spend time with her. After her first weeks in Hadleigh, people working in their gardens or out walking their dogs would greet her with a smile. Many stopped to have a friendly chat, encouraging her to believe that they had overcome any perception of her as different, as an interloper, and were, even in this short time, seeing her as someone already belonging to Home Farm and, hopefully, to the village.

As the weeks passed, it grew harder to leave each Monday morning and though she still enjoyed her work, the hours in the Cambridge office started to feel rather like an interlude in her real life. She bloomed. John said the country air was a beauty treatment for her. Physically fully recovered and as healthy as ever, she was also outgrowing her nervous fears but there were things still left undone that hovered disturbingly on the guilty edges of her mind. Since telling her mother that she would write, she had allowed the fact of having made one positive move to excuse her from doing more; the promise of action a substitute for anything actual. In Cambridge she thought about writing and told herself that she would have more time while at Hadleigh. In Hadleigh she found herself busier than expected and resolved to write when she was back in Cambridge. John, who was far more conscientious than she could bring herself to be, did keep in touch with her parents and had sent messages to both of them, explaining that, his grandmother having died, they were busily living two lives and trying to take care of his uncle. She relaxed a little and saw this as giving her a breathing space. If her mother heard nothing from her, she would understand the pressure she was under and would make allowances.

She was not constrained by lack of time. She was struggling with the difficulty of what and how to write. They had been cut off from each other for so long that it was hard to know what to say. There were unspoken reproaches on both sides to be either acknowledged or ignored. Deciding which line to take wasn't easy.

She was still in this troubled, indecisive state when her father made an intervention that brought everything about her interactions with her parents into sharper focus. He called one Saturday lunchtime. Maya had heard nothing of him since his recent visit though John, having told him about their new living arrangements, had given him the farmhouse number. It was John who answered the phone and called her over.

"It's your father. He has some news for you."

"Dad, how are you?" Maya screwed up her face at John as she listened to Peter's deep voice but her expression soon changed and she sat down on the nearest chair as if her legs would not hold her.

"Maya! Did you hear what I said?" Peter sounded irritated. "I'm getting married."

"When....who....? You aren't telling me that you are going to marry Karen?"

"Of course I am. Who else do you think it could be? That's why I wanted you to meet her when I came to see you. What's the matter with you? Why are you taking that tone? Didn't you like her?"

"She seemed pleasant enough. Rather younger than I expected. I didn't see her as anything more than a companion. It's a bit of a surprise to be asked to look on her as a stepmother." Maya could not help the acid creeping into her voice.

"I have known Karen for nearly a year now and we get on very well. We don't have any hang-ups over our age difference." Peter's voice hardened. "I thought you would be happy for me. I hope that you aren't going to be difficult over this."

"Are you really worried about what I think?" Maya's voice was cold. "You live your life now and I live mine. Have you told Mother what you are planning?"

"Don't pretend that you are concerned for your mother in this. Why should she mind what I do? We have been divorced for nine years. She lives a totally separate life and may well have friendships and plans of her own. I'm sure that you would not know anything about that. You know even less about her life than I do."

Maya's face was white and her mouth trembled. "Look. I'm going to pass you over to John. He will get all the details from you about when and where this will happen. Don't worry. He has made me promise to behave in a civilised way with you and mother but there is no point in our carrying on this conversation. We will upset each other badly. I need to take time to get used to what you've told me." Passing the phone to John, she ran out of the house.

Ten minutes later he found her where he had expected her to be, sitting in the gateway to the meadow. He sat down, put his arm round her shoulders and rested his cheek against hers.

"I know that you've had a nasty surprise but this is not so terrible. Your father is obviously lonely. Think of what it must be like having no-one share things with. You shouldn't be too hard on him."

"I'm sorry. I don't want to put you through another bout of my childish behaviour. I just need to adjust to the idea." She stifled an odd snort of laughter. "I've suddenly thought about my grandmother. She might have been upset to see her son's marriage break up, but from the start she had made Mother's life harder and was almost certainly pleased when she left for India. She never tried to hide her disapproval of Dad's choice and, though she tried to pretend otherwise, that was pure prejudice. Now, she's going to get her comeuppance. It's petty and mean, but think about her having to take on Karen."

"I think you should stop right there," John said discouragingly. "But at least you are reviving a bit. Do you want to know about the actual plans and dates involved?"

131

"No. Not straight away. Tell me later. One surprising thing is just how angry I feel on behalf of my mother. Still, I can hardly call anyone else to account for treating her badly. I've put off and put off writing to her. I will. I'll do it right now."

She turned to him and buried her face in his neck. "Oh John, whatever she was like, whatever I blame her for, to think of her being replaced by that Barbie doll. I can't bear it."

FOURTEEN

Bombay in the second week of September was not a particularly comfortable place to be. The monsoon was practically at an end but the atmosphere, as if reluctant to let it pass, held on to a few remnants of unshed rain and now hung over the city like a soggy, mildewed towel. If there were sporadic showers, they lasted briefly and the sky merely spat on the ground and wetted the dust for a few seconds. This did nothing to freshen the air but merely added a steamy slick to everything.

Nor was Soshan a particularly comfortable person to be with, as Mary frequently told her in less than servile tones. She was impatient and irritable. The artificial climate in the flat, comfortable as it was, had become something of a prison. She was tired of living like some cave creature in her air-conditioned rooms. She wanted to fling windows and doors open again. Mentally, too, she felt caged and cramped and on the verge of some wild outbreak. It did not help that Maya's promised and eagerly awaited letter had still not arrived.

The news of the miscarriage had been upsetting and raised worries about her health but it was the thought of Maya as a potential mother that was a bigger blow. It was a reminder of how much time had been lost. They might eventually achieve some sort of workable reconciliation – and there was at least a little better hope of that since their last telephone conversation – but there could be no more clinging to romantic and outworn dreams of missed opportunities made good. Her child was gone forever. She would have to negotiate with an unknown adult.

She felt lonely and unloved. She was often at odds with Mary; her parents had taken off for a belated holiday up in the northern hills; Sohrab had taken his daughters for a short stay with their mother's parents in Delhi. She had friends and did not lack invitations but she had no heart for being sociable. Waiting to hear from Maya was draining her of all initiative and, heavy-eyed and leaden, she was unable to act or move on until the expected, or more realistically the desired, breakthrough happened. As the month drew out, the weather improved slightly but her mood did not. Then, as the tension in the flat was at a point where Mary would slam her morning tea tray down on the bedside table and, forgoing her usual bout of tidying with its attendant gossip, stalk out of the room and start banging about in the kitchen, the longed for letter finally arrived. There it was, on the tray, with all her usual mail.

Home Farm,
Hadleigh,
Norfolk.
20/9/14

Mother,

I know that it is weeks since we spoke on the phone and that it has taken me too long to get round to writing this letter. I found it very hard to know what to say.

While it is not an excuse, I have been through an eventful three months. It started with your visit at the end of June. I've said sorry for the way I behaved but we both know that the unfortunate history between us is impossible to ignore. John is urging me to put it behind me and several things have happened recently to make me realise that holding on to old hurts will do none of us any good but even with the best of intentions, it isn't easy for me to let them go.

Then, in the first week of July, I had the miscarriage. It was painful and unpleasant but has done no lasting damage. There is no question of not having children in the future but that medical assessment isn't the point for me as I am not at all sure I want to take on motherhood. It could, as we know, end in disaster. Being a good mother isn't a given and the way I am, I have little faith that I would be one!

We had just recovered from this when we had to entertain Dad! Don't get in a state about that. He did not come to us in Cambridge but here to Hadleigh. The place was John's idea, the event was Dad's and you know how impossible it is to put him off doing anything he sets his mind to. He heard about us and London and had to have his day with me too. You see how hard we are going to have to work to escape all these leftover jealousies and conflicting egos. By the way, he brought a girlfriend with him. I don't know how you will feel about that.

All this was overshadowed by the death of John's grandmother on August 8th. She was ninety-three so though John and his mother are naturally sad, they can't be too grieved. However, because she had always lived with John's unmarried uncle and he has been so dependent on her all these years, losing her has left him alone and this has led to a considerable upheaval in our life. You'll see that I'm writing this while staying at his farm. We have been spending long weekends here for nearly two months now and are getting quite used to moving between two homes, but as we both love this place and in the end it will be his, John is considering the possibility of moving us here permanently. He just has to be sure that the farm can keep us all if he gives up his job. I would also change mine. It shouldn't be difficult to find something in this area. He is also considering using the farm in new ways. There are unused buildings that could be converted to high grade holiday lets. This would bring in additional money to partially compensate for his lost salary and hedge against future problems with a purely agricultural income. Sorry, I'm going into more detail than you want or need. I have got attached to the farm and am quite excited as we look at all the options. Everything is up in the air for now and there are no definite plans but I think that it is when, not if. We could even be here by Christmas.

John is looking far ahead and I know that he wants me to invite you here. This sounds like a great leap forward from where we are right now. I'll be honest. I'm still very doubtful about it. I'll be even more brutally honest. With you and Dad fighting over how I should be brought up, where I should belong, I feel incredibly lucky to have found myself someone and somewhere so

*solidly, so traditionally English and to have a chance of
a peaceful life in a place that I really like. I don't want
to carry any unwanted baggage forward into that. I do
though have to consider John's wishes. He wants me
to bring you and Dad into our lives. He feels that not
doing so will create unwanted baggage of its own. Let's
see how things go.*

*I said that Dad had brought a girlfriend with him when
he came to see us. I have no idea what sort of contact
you have with him or whether he has told you about
her. Has he let you know that he is going to marry her?
It was a surprise to me. I don't really like her. She is
around thirty and a bit silly. It's shattering to have to
think of her as a stepmother. They have set a wedding
date for the end of October. We shall have to go but
we won't see them too often after that. I wonder what
Granny Fielding thinks of the bride.*

*This has not been an easy letter. I may never feel as you
would like me to. Rejection is extremely hard to deal
with and it left me struggling to believe that anyone
would ever care about me. But John does. He wants us
all to be on good terms and I want to please him. Don't
rush me. I will be in touch again as soon as I know
what we are doing. I won't expect a reply. There isn't
really much more to say at the moment. It might be
best if you wait until I can give you more definite news.*

Maya

Soshan knew so little about Maya's current life that, on
opening this, she could hardly read it fast enough, eagerly
skimming off the obvious news. Only after her immediate

curiosity was satisfied, did she go through it again, very slowly, searching out the less overt messages, words and phrases that would tell her more about how Maya was feeling and thinking. These were not exactly hidden or difficult to find and in a way she was relieved to be faced with so many hurtful things so openly. For the moment this was better than the long silence she had endured. She instinctively fastened on the positive. Maya did seem to have recognised a need to change and to be aware that clinging to the past might put her future at risk. It was encouraging to be invited to share her obvious excitement about that future. Her pointed little gibe at Peter's mother even had a conspiratorial air. There was, though, no escape from the negative. It was chilling to share a daughter's clear-eyed look at her family and face her judgement of it as unwanted baggage. Seeing what had happened between them through Maya's eyes, no longer the eyes of a rebellious teenager but those of a troubled young woman, the full horror of it burst in on her. She had left her child unable to see herself as lovable and doubtful of her ability to love children of her own. Soshan was so paralysed by this vivid depiction of that legacy of emotional impairment that, without warning, with no breath, no sob or sound, tears simply flowed out of her and ran down her face.

"Your breakfast is ready." Mary's grumpy voice sounded in the passage and her unfriendly face, etched with the hostility of recent days appeared round the door. Her dour expression changed instantly and she gasped and rushed over to kneel on the floor beside the bed.

"No. Don't. Hush now. Don't." She took Soshan's hand and patted it frantically. "What is it? Please stop. We have had terrible time. I'm sorry to have been so mean with you.

138

Everything will be good. Don't cry. You never cry. Even when you were tiny, no crying. Always such a brave girl. What I can do? What I can bring you?" Mary's eyes too were now full of tears and her voice hoarse with emotion. "Tea is getting cold. I'll make fresh for you. Or better if I bring brandy."

Soshan, gently pushing Mary aside, got out of bed.

"No brandy. I would like fresh tea. I'll just wash my face and come outside onto the balcony for it. I'll be alright. It was this letter from Maya." She folded it and put it aside. "But this ridiculous behaviour won't do any good or change anything. Let's get ourselves back to normal."

By the time she had applied large amounts of cold water to her swollen eyes and brushed her hair she had regained her self-control. Mary, bringing the fresh tea out to where she was sitting on the balcony, had also calmed down. The two women said nothing for a while. Soshan drinking and Mary standing over her, examining her with forensic attention.

"Peter is getting married again." Soshan stared into her cup not wanting to see Mary's response.

"You cry over that man? You have much better man now."

"No, Mary. I'm not crying over that man. There were things Maya said that upset me but not that." She stood up. "I don't want breakfast yet. I'll have my bath first. I'll feel more myself then, more like eating something."

Half an hour later, as she came out of the bedroom again, bathed, dressed and largely restored, she saw Mary hastily put the phone down in the hall.

"I didn't hear it ring. Who was that calling?"

"Dr Wadia. Is coming. On his way to hospital." Mary sounded a little too offhand and there was a distinctly guilty look about her.

"That's odd." Soshan gave her a considering look. "He called late last night to say he was back from Delhi and would come here this evening."

"Well, is coming now." Mary sounded truculent.

"Mary! You called him didn't you? Really, sometimes you go too far."

"Very worried about you. You need someone. A poor old thing like me no good for you."

"A meddling old thing like you no good for me." She softened her harsh words with a small smile. "Go on. Get on with your work. I know you mean well. I'll forgive you."

Mary started on some household chores and Soshan went off to her study and tried to immerse herself in some paperwork but she was only half thinking about what she was doing and was alert for the sound of the doorbell. It wasn't long before Sohrab arrived and as he came into the room, Mary ostentatiously went off into her quarters and shut the door loudly. Soshan got up, came over to him and held out her arms in an unusually demonstrative gesture.

He held her tightly for a few seconds and then putting her away from him, looked at her enquiringly. "What is it? Mary says you have been crying. I gather from between the lines of what she said that you have been nervous and, to quote her, grumpy for days. I obviously don't want you to be miserable but I hope that means you've been missing me."

"Oh I have. You don't know how much." She kissed his cheek. "But that doesn't excuse me. I've been behaving badly. I've grown tired of this awful monsoon season. It has never bothered me so much before but Maya had said she would write to me and I've been waiting and waiting for her letter to come and the strain of that has simply made everything so much worse. Well, it came today. And there were devastating things in it. Look, here it is, you read it."

They sat together on a corner sofa and she leaned in close to him as he read. When he had finished, he passed the letter back and looked thoughtfully at her.

"So, Peter is remarrying. Does that upset you?"

"No! No!" She caught his hand and held it briefly to her lips. "You know how I feel about you. Peter is nothing anymore." She stroked his fingers. "Well, I have to be honest. It would give any woman a slight pang to think of the man she has lived with, had a child with, finding another woman. Especially if it's a younger woman. But that's pure vanity. When I think of the serious consequences of my ever having been involved with him, it's nothing."

"So we are back to Maya." He sounded weary.

"She is always there. You can see from what she says how badly I've damaged her. How can I allow myself to be happy knowing that?"

"You aren't allowing me to be happy either."

"Sohrab, I'm sorry, truly." Soshan looked so sad that he reached out for her again and she rested against him and let out an enormous breath. "I thought only of myself once before and I've paid for it. I can't seem to get over that even though I can see only too clearly, that by not thinking of you, I'm simply repeating an old mistake in a new form."

"Read that letter again, Soshan. Yes, Maya has emotional hang-ups. Yes, you were to a degree responsible for those, but see how many positive things emerge from what she has written. She has a good and loving husband. She is well on her way to living exactly the kind of life she has always felt deprived of. How many people have the chance to escape childhood misery in so perfectly suitable a fashion? She will be alright. Hopefully happiness will enable her to be forgiving but, whatever happens, you have to forgive yourself, or at least to understand that you can't be the only one in all this to lose any chance of a better future. Think again. Marry me."

She looked at him her face clouded with indecision and he took her by the shoulders and fixed her with an unwavering stare. "I have girls too. At the start of our friendship I worried about how they would feel if I replaced their mother. So our arrangement worked for both of us. It gave us physical comfort and companionship without too directly affecting our daughters. Now all those girls we were so concerned about are moving on, away from us, into lives of their own. Think carefully about what is ahead of us. We need more than this. We're getting older. We should be building something permanent now to last us; for us to rest on when we are really old. So I'm asking you again, marry me."

Soshan let out another huge breath. "I don't deserve you. I've missed you so much these last days while you were away. I've never felt so lonely before. It is getting harder and harder to be separated. I know that everything you say makes sense. I know you're right." She freed herself from his grasp and turned away from him, gazing unseeingly in front of her. Then, giving herself a shake, she turned back and said loudly, "Yes. Yes, Yes. I'll marry you."

"There's no need to act as if you are facing a firing squad." His voice trembled on the edge of laughter. He pulled her to her feet and they stood with their arms round each other, his head bent and his forehead resting on her hair until Soshan said worriedly, "This is happening too suddenly. I don't want you or other people to think that I am doing this because my ex-husband is getting a new wife. Perhaps we should wait."

Sohrab now laughed aloud and shook his head. "For a clever woman you can be very silly you know. What do I care what people think. But if it matters to you – and I certainly don't want to complicate your dealings with your ex-husband and daughter – we will wait. We'll announce what we're planning and you can write and tell Maya and Peter but we'll wait. We'll take time to organise everything properly and everyone will have a chance to get used to the idea." He looked at his watch. "Speaking of time, this is terrible timing but I must leave you now." He ruffled her hair and pulled a humorous face. "This was after all an emergency call. A very successful one as you will agree but I simply have to get to the hospital. I'm late already. I'll come back early this evening. We can write your letters together, then we'll go out for a celebratory dinner."

This is what they did and two carefully worded letters with a good deal of input from Sohrab were sent off to England. Their news delighted their families and closest friends in India and Sohrab's daughters kissed him and hugged Soshan making it very clear just how pleased they were. It did not escape her that they were actually rather relieved by this new-found freedom to go ahead with their own plans, unworried by any feelings of responsibility for their father's happiness. She had to acknowledge just how right he had been about their moving on and could only hope that Maya was in the same state of mind.

Mary positively bounced around the flat, full of herself, sure that in calling Sohrab she had finally brought about the thing that she had been campaigning for so long and so assiduously.

"Yes. Yes." Soshan said affectionately. "You are a real matchmaker. I owe it all to you."

FIFTEEN

Maya, conscious of being totally unreasonable and failing to live up to her newly-minted resolutions, was extremely irritated when she received the letter from her mother. It lay on the breakfast table beside her and glaring at it, she bit noisily and aggressively into her toast as if she were visualising herself destroying the thing unopened.

If the previous three months had been eventful, the next three did not promise to be much less so. Faced with a major physical upheaval in her life, she was unwilling, unable even, to pay much attention to the emotional upheavals that had tormented her and taken up so much of her energy for so long. For now at least, these had lost their immediacy.

She and John were still making their regular and tiring transitions and had reached Hadleigh late the previous evening after a long, slow journey through exceptionally heavy traffic. This would all soon be over. John and Robert having finally agreed that it would be viable for them to join forces, they were moving permanently to the farm at the beginning of November. Maya planned to leave her job at the end of October and was already looking for another nearby, while John would continue to travel daily into Cambridge until he had worked out his three months notice at the laboratory.

She had taken it for granted that in asking her mother not to send a reply but to wait for more news, she had deferred any further development in their disjointed dialogue and bought herself time. She had expected to set the pace and take charge of the timetable for their tentative reconciliation. Like a badly behaved, thwarted toddler, she crunched fiercely on in a shower of toast crumbs, the letter still unread, until a mental image of an invitation card from her father, a heavily embossed, conventional aggravation that had arrived a few days earlier, jolted her out of this childish behaviour. In her heart she knew that, by accepting this invitation, she was giving him more leeway than she had ever allowed her mother. She had always unfairly expected less of him and been less hurt by anything he did. Wiping her mouth and fingers on her napkin, she picked the letter up and roughly tore it open.

Bombay
27/9/14

Dear Maya,

It was both reassuring and disturbing in almost equal measure to read your letter. And I'd like to say that if this is an old-fashioned way to communicate, there is something really satisfying about holding something so ACTUAL from you in my hand. I don't want to dwell on the sadder elements in it. The good thing was to hear that you are embarking on a life that you look forward to, in a place that feels like home. It was interesting to learn about the farm and your plans for living there. I did not know about your father's girlfriend but I'm truly glad to hear that he has a new person in his life. I should have told you that I, too, have someone and I will tell you more about him in a moment.

What really struck me, and finally made me decide to write this letter, was that we have all come to a pivotal moment in our lives. It felt like one to me when I came back to India and left you with your father, but that was more of an unconsidered response to an impossible situation. I went away but I did not really leave. I have trailed the past and all that I did wrong in it behind me like a bedraggled skirt hem all these years. It has held me back and made me inflict further hurt on yet more people. I hope that you will do better than I have and not inflict your pain on anyone in the same way. You, your father and I are survivors of a joint disaster but, as we are all about to make a fresh start, we can hopefully, if not forget our past, remember it in a new and more forgiving spirit. Your future looks set to give you all that you need, all that you have been feeling deprived of. I so much want that for you. Enjoy it wholeheartedly, without any backward looks.

Now, about my friend. His name is Sohrab, Dr Sohrab Wadia. He is also a Parsi, a successful doctor and a widower with two daughters and he has asked me to marry him. He is four years older than I am and lost his wife to cancer six years ago. When she died, his daughters, Kerman and Persis, were eleven and thirteen years old. Among several reasons for my hesitating to accept him all this time was my fear of hurting either you or them. I did not want you to feel I was replacing you, or them to feel that I was replacing

147

their mother but Sohrab has finally persuaded me that we shall now, inevitably, become less important to you all. Persis finished school last year and is doing a course in textile design at one of the excellent art schools here in the city, while her younger sister, Kerman, has to finish a final year of school and then hopes to study in England or America. All this together with your news makes me feel that Sohrab is right. I have said that I will marry him and we are thinking about setting a date in March or April next year. I would very much like you to meet him before that. Your time between now and Christmas will be much taken up with all the changes you are making so we thought that we might come to England together in early January. I understand your hesitation about inviting me to stay with you but please consider coming to see us in London and perhaps staying there for a few days this time.

I have written to your father and sent him good wishes and told him my news. I am pleased that you will be going to his wedding. Perhaps you will get to like his new wife in time but that isn't really important, is it? You can overcome the wrongs we did you by leading a satisfactory life of your own. Don't let the past entrap you into future problems.

With much love

Mother

At that moment John, who had gone out with Robert after an unusually early breakfast, came into the room and peered into the coffee pot. "Oh good there's still some left. We've done the rounds. Uncle is in the office with a friend who's just dropped by and wants to take him off to see something on his own farm. I'm not needed anymore. I'm yours for the rest of the day."

When she didn't answer, he turned and gave her his full attention for the first time since coming indoors. "What is it? You look a bit tense."

"It's this." Maya waved the letter at him. "It's from Mother, as you probably saw earlier. It appears that she is getting married too. No weddings all these years and suddenly two come along at once. You'd better read it. She has quite a lot to say." Her mouth twisted sardonically. "Quite a lot of advice to give."

John read it through carefully and gave it back to her. "It's extremely good advice. I can see that you don't like her telling you what to do but, as she says, she only wants you to be happy." His voice deepened. "You *are* happy?"

"You know I am. I don't feel like the same girl. Only a short time ago, just having you seemed like more than I could have ever asked for and I was always afraid that I might lose you. Now, I not only have you, I have this place. But the real miracle is that I'm free of all that weight of worry I was carrying. Well, it's not a miracle. It was sharing everything with you that did it. That feels good."

"So why cling on to attitudes that could spoil everything? Your mother is right. Even if you can't forget all that has happened, remembering it in a new way would let you out of a sort of prison. Your parents are both planning a new future. Let that free us, free you, to move forward unencumbered into ours."

Maya longed to do as he said, but etched on her heart, too deeply ever to be completely eradicated, was the primal fear and misery that only a small child confronted with powerful, angry adults can know and she was still struggling against an unsatisfied urge for reparation, an insistent need to see someone pay for all that she had suffered.

The thought that those two unknown girls, Kerman and Persis, would soon be living with her mother, that she would be their stepmother, that they would be a family, re-ignited a bitterness she had believed she was slowly overcoming. How did they feel about all this? It was impossible to decide if their bereavement, their mother not only no longer with them, but nowhere and gone forever, was harder than her loss, her mother living, but living elsewhere, careless of her. It was all too complicated, too much for her right now. She would not answer this letter for a while. She would focus on getting through her father's wedding. Sending news of that would be an innocuous reason for writing again.

She decided, as a matter of pride, to make a special effort for the occasion and began searching for a suitable outfit. She was a casual dresser and had never been particularly interested in fashion but she saw this as demanding something more of her. Karen would have to be shown that she was not the only one who could shop successfully or be glamorous.

The invitation had, strictly speaking, been sent by Karen's parents but Maya understood that they both worked in unexceptional jobs and thought that Peter was probably paying most of the costs of the affair, a combined civil ceremony and reception at a smart, expensive riverside hotel in Berkshire, not far from his house.

They were lucky in the weather. Though it was late October, the sun shone, it was pleasantly mild and while there was a breeze, it was not strong enough to make exuberant hats unmanageable. As they arrived the hundred and fifty elegantly dressed guests were served champagne and canapés on the long terrace facing the river and once they were all assembled, led to rows of white wicker chairs set out in the hotel orangery among lush greenery and extravagant floral displays. The registrar was already in place at the far end of the room, behind a table draped in white and decorated with a further elaborate flower arrangement in a silver vase. Peter, magnificent in morning dress, was talking quietly to him but as a burst of recorded music announced the appearance of the bride, he turned. Karen, slender in fitted white lace, her tanned shoulders shown to advantage by a halter neckline, entered through a far door and came slowly towards him, the heady perfume from her bouquet of lilies wafting over the seated congregation.

In contrast to the lavishness of the surroundings, the ceremony was short and simple and the vows as plain as they could be. After it was over and they had signed the register to the strains of more music, Karen and Peter left the orangery and waited just outside the door of the large dining room to greet everyone as they were ushered through to their tables.

"Maya, darling, you look gorgeous." Karen's voice was high and excited and her carefully tinted cheeks were beginning to glow with a more hectic pink. "And what a great hairdo."

Maya, dazzling in a silk maxi dress and strappy sandals, with a matching fascinator pinned in her carefully arranged hair, gave her father a perfunctory kiss and her lips brushed through the air just clear of Karen's face.

With so many guests, conversations, either in the reception line or over lunch, were desultory and inconsequential. Maya and John sat at the top table with the bridal couple, Peter's mother, the bride's parents, her two sisters and their husbands. Peter and Karen, distracted by the role they were playing to a large audience, devoted most of any attention they could spare from this performance to his mother and her parents. After the meal they went off on a long convivial tour of the room before posing for photographs next to a three-tiered cake decorated in silver and white and making the traditional first cut into this. Then as the waiters took over and began serving it with coffee, they left everyone happily concentrating on food again and went up to a hotel room to change for their journey to some unspecified destination. A few guests who had travelled long distances had been booked into rooms at the hotel and would be having dinner there, but no evening function had been arranged and after waving the couple off, people began to disperse and the whole thing was over.

Maya and John were staying overnight. Escaping the farewells and final burst of excitement and looking for some peace, they went into a nearby lounge where they found Peter's mother sitting by herself in a far corner. Bravely outfacing any disquiet she might be feeling, Mrs Fielding had sailed through the occasion in a fuchsia suit that denied her eighty years and shouted celebration. Any reservations she might have about her new daughter-in-law had been concealed under a matching, wide-brimmed hat. This now lay on a chair beside her and she was revealed as pale and tired, her eyes drooping with fatigue and her mouth a little tremulous.

Maya, her heart unexpectedly pinched, went over to her grandmother and said gently, "Granny, I know we are full of food and drink but it might be nice to have a cup of tea. John's mother calls that the answer to all life's problems."

"Karen's parents will be here any minute. They are driving me back. No time for tea."

"They can always wait. If you would like tea, have it."

"Perhaps not, dear. My metabolism is not as efficient as it was and even if it's not a long journey, the company will be trial enough. I don't want to add physical discomfort to that."

Maya had forgotten that her grandmother could be so acerbic, never hesitating to speak frankly about subjects that other people might avoid.

"I haven't seen or heard from you since you left your father's house, Maya. I've missed you. I was hurt that you didn't ask me to your wedding." Mrs Fielding looked a little sour but her expression softened as she turned and smiled at John who came and sat down on the other side of her. "It was sad never to have met this very likeable husband of yours till now."

Maya flushed, suddenly ashamed of her rejection of someone who, despite her faults, had cared for her for so long. "There were no guests. It was a very short and simple affair. Only Dad and John's mother were there. We didn't want any fuss."

"Yes, well maybe that was wise. At least you seem to have got the basics right. I am very taken with this young man." She patted John's hand and shot her granddaughter a wry look. "You have been either sensible or lucky. Your father has certainly made a considerable fuss here today, though

I suspect that the more elaborate details were likely to have been Karen's choice. As to the basics, well, he never gets those right." She saw Maya's face darken. "Yes, I know. I behaved badly over your mother. But I saw from the start that it was a mistake for both of them." She shook her head, her lips pursed. "He is my son and maybe I shouldn't say this, but though he is a good man in many ways, he is a hard man and not a giver. Where I am concerned he is always dutiful but not affectionate. Soshan had sacrificed a great deal for him and he was never going to give her all she needed to make up for that. It was a disaster and, unfortunately, not only for them." She sat back in her chair and rested her head for a moment, her eyes hooded.

John looked at Maya his brows raised but suddenly found himself tapped on the arm. "This child had a hard time. I know she blames me for a great deal. With some justification maybe, but I was thrust into a situation that was not of my making, you know, and I did the best I could." She turned to Maya. "Your mother was very young and had lived a very privileged life. She was full of romantic ideas and reality was a bit of a shock for her. She could be extremely trying. Listening to her comments on England and the English I often felt under attack, though I realised that these were just substitutes for her real grievances. Well it's over. I only hope that it is over for you and that you will be able to put it all behind you and build a satisfactory life with this husband of yours. As for your father, there is no pretence of love to muddy the waters this time. Karen will do whatever Peter asks as long as he gives her the things she wants and it's fairly clear what those are. She is being realistic and so I suppose is he. It should work. I don't expect much from her or to see much of her." She shot Maya a shrewd look. "I daresay you think I'm getting what I deserve. Well, again you may be right but I would like to think that you can be kind and that I might see something of you again. It could soon be too late."

Before Maya could answer, John hastily intervened, "As I told you over lunch, we are about to move and we need to give my uncle, whose home we'll be sharing, time to get used to living with us, but it would be good to have you to stay with us once that is all sorted. It might anyway be best to wait for the spring and better weather since we are so rural. Bad weather in the countryside always seems harsher than in town. Maya will write to you and arrange something."

At that moment Karen's parents came bustling in and again Maya had no chance to say anything in response.

"There you all are. We're just about to leave, Mrs Fielding. Are you ready to go?"

Karen's father was short, round and red-faced and beginning to look uncomfortable in his formal suit. Her mother, slight and slim as her daughter, was smart in a tight-skirted dress and jacket but beneath heavy make-up her face was lined, her mouth thinning and her eyes tired. Maya had uncharitable thoughts about how Karen might look after a few years.

"I just need to go to the cloakroom and then I'm ready." Her grandmother struggled out of her chair. "I shall be glad to get home. I'm very grateful to you for taking me."

"Not at all. It's no trouble. Peter has entrusted you to us and we are glad to be useful."

Once they had seen the rather weary trio to their car and waved them goodbye, John turned to Maya and said, "Well, that was a surprise. Your grandmother isn't at all what I expected. She seems to be a very sensible and shrewd old lady. And brave with it."

"Does that mean you don't believe what I've told you about her? She *was* prejudiced you know, most people are without even realising it. Your mother has admitted to being bothered by my looks and origins and she is also sensible and shrewd and brave with it."

"Of course I believe you. I believe that's the way it was for you. I also admit that you are probably right about the prejudice. But you were a child after all. You saw what happened from that perspective. Other people saw things differently. That's normal. That's why it's always possible to look at anything in a new way. Think of seeing an old film again after a long time. You liked it at first viewing, but the second time around it isn't as exciting or as moving, or even as good, as you remembered it. The film hasn't changed, you have."

Maya lightly punched his arm and, for the first time ever, sounded more than a little cross with him. "Why are you always so rational and reasonable....and right?"

"I thought you liked me that way."

"I love you. Most of the time I like you. It's just that it's getting hard to be put in the wrong so often. Knowing that I usually am only makes it worse."

"I suppose that I became an adult too soon. When my father died, I felt I had to take over where Mother was concerned so I didn't have any chance to sow any wild oats or be a normal teenager. I became serious overnight and stayed that way."

He pulled a face and looked downcast but he was actually encouraged by the fact that Maya was now ready to criticise him, however mildly. It was, in an unspectacular way, a tremendous step forward. He put his arm round her and said mischievously, "Actually, I did have a few months of madness when I first started living alone but I'm not going to tell you anything about those. I'll hang on to a little mystery and perhaps you won't see me as such an old sober-sides. Come on, let's get out of all this formal gear and go for a walk along the river and when we get back perhaps I'll show you my wild side."

SIXTEEN

At the end of October Maya's colleagues organised a leaving party for her at which addresses and promises to keep in touch were exchanged. She did hope to get to Cambridge from time to time and catch up with them all, but knew that as time went on they would inevitably begin to drift apart.

She had found a new job as a secretary-cum-receptionist at the primary school in a neighbouring village. It would not be far from the farm and would be more closely interwoven with her life than her previous one. She had really wanted it and, getting ready for her interview, had peered critically at herself in the mirror and frowned discontentedly at the fair-skinned, but distinctly eastern-looking, young woman who stared back at her. She had been worried that her appearance might count against her in such a rural and predominantly English establishment. Now, she concluded, with a degree of cynicism, that it might have helped. The school could be seen as inclusive while still getting a local with impeccable local connections.

She shook off these unkind, negative thoughts. She was very lucky. The post had many advantages: as she would be working at the school to which all the younger Hadleigh children went, it would bring her into contact with people in their own village; as it was not vacant until after the

Christmas holiday and she would be starting in the first week of January, she could concentrate on re-organising her domestic affairs before she took on this new assignment; the hours, eight to four-fifteen, and the long holidays would leave her considerable freedom to help John with his rental project. The greatest benefit for her personally was that, while mainly using her administrative and IT skills, the additional responsibility of acting as a receptionist would mean coming face to face with parents and school visitors and her work would be considerably more varied and less isolated than in the Cambridge office.

She did not, in fact, need much time to prepare for the house-move. Their furniture was minimal, very basic, so new that they had not yet become attached to it and, the farmhouse being already fully furnished, there was no actual need for any of it.

This had worried John. "Most women like to choose their own decor and furnishings. Are you okay with moving into somewhere set up by other people and untouched in some places for years?"

"That's what I love about it. It's so solid, secure. It has lasted, survived." Maya struggled to articulate just how reassuring all this was to someone as insecure, as unanchored as she had always been. She tried to set his mind at rest. "Maybe we could paint the bedroom, put up our own pictures and use our bed linen. I did take some trouble over choosing that. The rest of the house is fine and there's no hurry to alter even our room. All I really care about are my books and the bureau that you bought me for my birthday and we'll find a place for them somewhere."

Since there was ample storage space in the buildings he wanted to convert, John decided to keep their furniture and use it as a starter for his planned cottages. On arrival at the farm, everything could be unloaded into one of these and the few things they intended to use taken into the main house slowly over the following few days.

This accommodating attitude, the minimal disruption and the speed with which the whole business was to be accomplished greatly heartened Robert. Uneasily aware that he had gone downhill physically since the death of his mother, he was torn between relief at having John to help him out and a distinct wariness at the thought of Maya's permanent presence. He did realise, though, that she might well be far less troubling to have around than his sister who had been his reluctant companion in the evenings all this time. Their differences had not lessened with age and on several occasions they had only narrowly avoided an outright quarrel.

"I hope you are going to behave well with Maya." This was not the first lecture that Joyce had subjected him to. "You were very slow to come to terms with her. You of all people should know better than to be judgemental about others."

"I don't know what on earth you mean by that." Robert had flushed an angry red and hit back. "And don't pretend that you were overjoyed about her at first. You took your time to get to like her."

"I admit that. I was wrong. I should have trusted John's judgement. They have their problems. Maya didn't have an ideal childhood and she can be a bit unpredictable but that isn't entirely down to her unusual background. There are people that we've known for years who have their quirks. I can see that she and John will be good for each other and you are more than lucky that they are going to take care of you. Make sure that you treat her kindly."

Joyce was well aware of just how lucky she was. She would soon be free of the demanding and unwelcome duty of keeping Robert company, which she found physically, as well as emotionally exhausting. John was coming, if not back to her, back to Hadleigh and Maya, who had caused her so much worry and heart-burning, was proving to be an exemplary daughter-in-law. It was unlikely that any of the girls she had previously pictured in that role would have been so relaxed about living as a newly-wed with a frail and unarguably crotchety old man; an old man, moreover, who would see the home she was to take on as his rather than hers. Grateful for the way things were turning out, she had tried to think of how Maya could be given a better deal than she appeared to be getting and suddenly recalled her fascination with the room that had been Iva's retreat. It would be a generous gesture to make it over to her and leave her free to do what she liked in the one part of the house where Robert had never been allowed and which he had always considered off limits. Fortunately, though at first inclined to be tetchy, the thought that Maya would have a separate room and they would be able to spend time apart overcame his reluctance to change anything associated with his mother, indeed any doubts he might have had about change of any kind, and he raised no longstanding objections to this plan. When John enthusiastically agreed that it was a great idea, Joyce offered to sort out and dispose of all Iva's belongings so that the totally empty room could be presented to Maya as a welcome gift on the day that she arrived.

She cleared the photographs off the walls, disposing of those that meant nothing to either her or Robert. She kept many of Iva and Nathan and themselves at various stages of their lives, putting a few of them on odd wall spaces in the passageways, taking others to the cottage and storing the rest. The embroidery materials, the tapestry cushions, the sewing machine and the old table and chair were given to charity.

If she had a momentary pang at this summary disposal of her mother's belongings, this final obliteration of her presence, Joyce concentrated on the future and, after two hard days, surveyed the result of her work with tired satisfaction. She felt that she had done something worthwhile for Maya, something that allowed her to express a growing affection for her in a subtle and useful way.

The removal van and John's car reached the farm at midday on the first of November. At two o'clock, when the van had been unloaded and the few immediately necessary boxes and suitcases containing clothing and toiletries had been taken upstairs, Joyce joined them all for a late, light lunch and was with them when John opened the small door in the dining room with a flourish and showed Maya the unadorned space inside.

"Here you are. This is officially your room. It's our present to you. It was Mum's idea. She knows that you like it and that you understand what it meant to Gran." He glanced briefly at his uncle. "Robert is pleased that, like her, you will have somewhere in this old house that is your own. You can decorate and use it as you like. It's our thank you for being ready to take us all on."

Maya stood looking into the room. She remembered her guilty inspection of it the morning after Iva's death and the moments she had shared there with Joyce after the funeral. She had to hold back tears. "No-one has to thank me for anything. It's wonderful to be here. Joyce is right, I was taken by this room from the start. I shall really enjoy organising and using it. It's a perfect present."

By the middle of December normality and routine had been more or less established, though, as John was still working in Cambridge until the end of that month and was away from seven-thirty in the morning until after six in the evening and Maya had not yet started her new job, further changes would be necessary in the new year. Legal arrangements had been made, under which, effectively, Robert would be employing John as Farm Manager. It remained to be seen how he would cope with having less work and responsibility and whether having more spare time would make him insecure and more troublesome to live with. Meanwhile, he was out of the house most of the day and the evenings were much the same as they had been over their long weekends together.

Mrs Hemsby, who on hearing that John and Maya were moving in permanently had confided in Joyce that she did not know how she would get along with a foreigner telling her what to do, was carrying on as before. Far sooner than had seemed likely, she appeared oblivious to any apparent difference she had once been aware of in Maya and saw only John's friendly and pretty wife. She was not exactly chatty and forthcoming but that was hardly her way and she accepted Maya's supervision of the planning and preparing of meals with no obvious discontent.

John had found a local man to paint Maya's room, as they now called it, and to fix shelves on two of the walls. Her books and attractive antique bureau had found a perfect home and she added a reclining chair and coffee table retrieved from their Cambridge furniture, which she put under the window where Iva had once sat. Unlike her predecessor, she had no urge to escape from her role as Mrs Carter and be simply Maya. There was nothing simple about that character. Still, if she did not yet feel the need of a retreat, this was the first place that had ever been entirely hers and it was very agreeable to be alone in it.

They had a quiet Christmas. They went to the carol service in the church and, because traditionally the family had always done so, to midnight mass. Joyce came back to the farm with them after this and stayed for two nights. She had shown Maya where the old, indeed ancient, carefully hoarded, Christmas baubles were kept and together they had decorated a small tree and put it in the dining room. They opened the presents that had been placed under it, after lunch on Christmas day. There were no elaborate or expensive items. They were all treading carefully, holding their breath, and their fire, until this new regime was absolutely, unquestionably, up and running.

Alone that night in their still unaltered bedroom, John and Maya exchanged a long kiss. Slightly breathless, he held her away from him and looked at her searchingly.

"Are you alright? Is this going to work? I have seen only too little of you in the last weeks. Is Robert behaving well? Do you find him peculiar? I know it's a bit late to ask all these questions and there's no going back, but if you have any worries, if anything upsets you, I need to know and try to sort things out."

"Everything is fine. I'm fine. I'm really looking forward to starting at the school. As for Robert, I feel so sorry for him that I can forgive any oddities in his behaviour. He's such a lonely man and he has lost the only person who ever loved him. It wrings my heart. I want to do all we can for him." She bit her lip, hesitated and then said contritely, "It's still my old life that is the one dark spot. I have to get in touch with Mother again. We'll have to meet this new man of hers and I am finding the thought of that unnerving. I can see that she has to get on with her life like the rest of us but, however hard I try, I still feel some resentment when I think of her walking away from what she did to me."

"If you can sympathise with Robert, you should try to see your mother in the same way. Someone hurt and lonely. I'm becoming a bore on this but I can't say it often enough. Try to see the past as it must have been for other people. Not for their sake, but for yours and mine."

"I know. I know." She rubbed her cheek against his. "I am going to make an all-out effort. We'll meet Mother and her doctor in London when they come next month. It's not ideal at the start of a new job, but if I can take even one day off, we could spend some time there. I'll behave beautifully." Then her head drooped and her voice quivered, "It's just that, even though remembering what happened to me isn't quite as bad as before, deep inside me there's this tiny childish voice saying, 'It's not fair! It's not fair!'"

"Well, no, it isn't fair. Were all the things that happened to my mother fair? Was losing my father fair?" John hugged her. "Sorry. Sorry. I'm turning into Mr Sober-sides again. I do know how tough it has been for you but you've come a long way in the last months and I think you can silence that small voice. You are a lot braver and more generous than you realise."

SEVENTEEN

The first two weeks of January offered pick-and-mix weather. There were very mild, sunny days, dark, gloomy ones and intermittent gales, with news reports of falling trees and police warnings to take care while driving. Maya was glad that John was no longer doing the Cambridge run. He was, though, taking her to work and collecting her at the end of her day. They agreed that she needed to learn to drive and be able to get about independently but since his schedule could be arranged largely as he pleased and it was only a ten minute journey to the school, this seemed for the time being a workable arrangement. He wanted her to be comfortable in her new life before she took on anything further.

By the middle of the month this daily ride was woven seamlessly into the fabric of her days and she had got to grips with her work. She was hardworking and conscientious and even before starting the job, had been given some time to go through it with the outgoing secretary and had spent considerably more absorbing background information from leaflets and the internet. The staff had welcomed her warmly. Coming from the surrounding villages and more fixed in their lives and ways than her mobile, transient Cambridge colleagues, these women – for it was a totally female workforce – were, nevertheless, more open to the outside world than Maya herself. One of the younger teachers had recently been on holiday in Thailand and two of the teaching assistants talked enthusiastically about their gap years in India. She had to admit, rather shamefacedly, that she knew less about the country than they did. Yes, her mother was Indian and she had an Indian family but she had no contact with them.

Sensing that there might be some troubled history behind this, they talked about other things. She was grateful for their tact but could not resist the rather snide thought that for all their travels and enthusiasm for far-flung countries, they might be said to view the world as a vast Disneyland provided for their enjoyment and entertainment. Did they know that much more than she did about actual Indian lives? Such criticism, even if justified, did nothing to lessen her discomfort at being exposed as narrow and insular. She resolved to become more informed about her mother's country and the community that she belonged to. There were plenty of books available. Her determined ignorance was proving embarrassing. She was no longer a child. There was no excuse for it. She had to live in the world as it was, as an adult.

Sooner than expected she was beginning to know most of the children and to recognise some of their parents, all of whom appeared to take her in their stride. Robert and John could tell her more about these people. They had known many of them for years, had shared their own schooling with either them or their parents. This direct and daily contact with old connections of his marked another milestone in her dealings with Robert. They now had things of common interest to talk about but though she spent some evenings with the men, she often went off into her room where she had installed a television and could watch programmes that they had no interest in.

Joyce, who still had concerns about Maya, had offered to reverse her previous weekday role and take over for them as Robert's companion for the occasional weekend.

"She is too young to be living such a dull life," she told John forcefully. "And you both need a bit of privacy. Take her away for some time on your own together. Go to Norwich. Or Cambridge. Maybe the coast. Find a good hotel. Eat out. Go to the theatre."

"I will, Mum. But this trip to London is rather hanging over us. We'll deal with that first. Then, I promise, we'll arrange a regular weekend off each month. Thanks for offering to help."

Soshan had sent messages to say that she and Sohrab had fixed on the tenth of April as a suitable wedding date. They had checked that Maya should be having her Easter holiday then and be free to come to India. They very much hoped that she would. There was not that much time and if she decided to come, all sorts of decisions had to be made. Their London visit had been delayed but they had now booked their flight and hotel and were due to arrive on Thursday the fifth of February. Hopefully this minor postponement would at least mean that the weather in England would have marginally improved. Apparently, the last two weeks of January were expected to be freezing cold and there could even be disruption at the airport.

Maya, having made up her mind to see this through, replied that she and John would be with them sometime on the Friday and would leave after lunch on Sunday. If she had its name, it would make sense for them to stay at the same hotel.

Soshan's final message, besides giving details of the hotel, informed them of her surprise plan for a lunch party on the Saturday. She had invited Peter, Karen and Granny Fielding to join them and also an Indian friend who worked in London called Mariam Thomas. This was someone she very much wanted everyone to meet and it might be good to have an outsider to lighten any possible tensions and make them all behave. If they didn't, Mariam, an experienced doctor who had dealt for many years with varied and sometimes difficult patients, would no doubt take that in her stride.

It seemed to Maya that the days now passed more quickly than usual and before she was totally ready for it the London weekend was upon them. Joyce came in on the Friday morning with all she needed to see her through the next two days and Maya having asked to leave work at lunchtime, they were on their way by three that afternoon, hoping to be in London by seven at the latest.

At eight o'clock that evening, a call made to Soshan to inform her of their arrival, their bags unpacked and the two of them bathed and dressed for what was for both of them a special occasion, they entered the softly-lit hotel dining room and were directed to a far table.

"There you are." Soshan, striking in a blue silk sari, as if this time around she was making no apology for her Indian identity, rose to greet them and gestured at the tall, slim man who stood up beside her. "Maya this is Sohrab. Sohrab, Maya and her husband, John."

"Maya. John. It's a pleasure to meet you at last." Sohrab smiling at them, indicated the chairs opposite himself and Soshan and sat down again.

Disconcerted by this combination of coolness and formality, Maya sat for a few moments without saying anything until, picking up a bottle already there beside him, Sohrab asked her if she would like a glass of wine.

"Yes. Thank you." She looked up at him and was taken aback by the appraising look she caught on his face before he turned away to pour her wine and offer some to John.

They were all silent for a while, sipping their drinks, gathering themselves to take the conversation forward. Soshan spoke first, leaning towards John and almost overwhelming him with a spate of questions about the farm, about how things were going, how he was dealing with the loss of his previous job and about his plans for the future. Maya, excluded and ignored by her mother who seemed determined to risk no rebuff from her, was left to Sohrab.

"You know," he said thoughtfully, "this, for me, is a similar experience to that of seeing on film, a character from fiction whose appearance and personality are very real to me. Cinematically made flesh you might say. Usually the film version doesn't match my mental picture at all." He saw her startled expression. "Well, Maya, I have, of course, seen photographs taken at various stages of your life, but the vivid image that I have of you rests mainly on what I have heard about you from your mother. You have been the central character in her story and, by association, very important in mine." He looked directly into her eyes and said quietly, "You and your mother have been equally affected by what you have both suffered. She only finally agreed to marry me because she can see that you have a good life ahead of you with John and, to an extent, this has freed her from anxiety and guilt. I'm sorry that, as a child, you had to go through so much but I want you to be clear that my main concern is that she should, at last, be free of all that."

Maya tore her eyes from his penetrating gaze and picked up her glass. She went to take a sip of wine but her hand was trembling and a few drops spilt on the cloth. She felt John's warm clasp as he took the glass from her and set it on the table.

"I think you should have some food, sweetheart, before drinking any more. You are very tired." He gave Sohrab a warning frown. "She was working all morning and the drive through Friday traffic was rather manic. We're not used to such aggression."

"We should have been more thoughtful. We're too used to eating at ridiculously late hours in Bombay." Soshan, clearly taken aback by overhearing what Sohrab had seen fit to say so early in their evening, gave him a sharp rap on the arm. "Let's order."

"I'm sorry." Sohrab turned, first to her and then to John. His apology, like their preceding remarks, had subtle overtones. "Of course we should eat." He beckoned a waiter.

Taking time out to study menus in the neutral presence of the waiter allowed them all to recover and once they had ordered, Sohrab looked at Maya. "I'm sorry to have upset you." His voice was firm but his eyes kind. "I have daughters who are only a little younger than you and should have known better than to be so direct, so harsh. Yet it is important that we face realities. We can't waste time on insincere platitudes. It matters a great deal to me that we should be friends but any worthwhile friendship is based on honesty. Tomorrow I shall meet your father, his new wife and your grandmother but they, it must be said, are no longer really important. It is the four of us here tonight who will share a future. We need to clear away the sad debris of the past. To do that we shall need your help."

John moved closer to Maya and she could feel his thigh against hers, a reminder that she wasn't alone in facing these frank demands on her. "I'm here, Sohrab. That's a sort of declaration of intent." Her lip quivered, "I can see, though, that Mother is finding it hard to believe that I will behave myself and can't even risk talking to me because I acted so outrageously the last time we were together." She drew a breath and said firmly, "You want honesty. Well, I don't think I can forget the past or sweep it away as you suggest. It can, and does, still hurt me but I am trying to do what everyone keeps asking me to do, remember it more forgivingly. I do truly hope that you will both be happy."

Soshan, her eyes bright with unshed tears, got up and, coming round behind her, fleetingly brushed the back of her neck with her fingertips. "I'm so sorry for everything darling. You don't know how sorry. But I'm glad that you have found this lovely man. He will make up to you for so much." Her cheeks were suddenly damp. "Excuse me. I just have to go to the cloakroom." She walked hastily away.

"Do you want to go and see that she is alright?" John's voice was a little unsteady.

Maya shook her head without replying and drank more wine as if swallowing something hard in her throat.

When Soshan returned, her face repaired and her poise intact, Sohrab smiled apologetically at her. "Perhaps that is enough plain talk and raw emotion," he spoke gently. "We have probably said all that needed saying for now. I think we know where we stand and should ease back a little. Look! I can see our food coming. Let's do our best to make this an enjoyable meal. Give ourselves some respite. We still have hurdles ahead. Tomorrow's lunch may not be plain sailing. Maya, let me tell you a little about my daughters. It may seem odd to you but they will, in a sense, be your sisters." He ignored her involuntary intake of breath. "They are very anxious to meet you. I hope that will happen soon. On the tenth of April certainly or, better still, before that. Soshan can explain later what we are planning and discuss the practicalities of your coming out to be with us."

He launched them on a lighter, more general conversation by telling them what his daughters were currently doing and outlining their future plans. While not explicitly praising their courage in coping with the loss of their mother, he certainly conveyed an impression of them as having made an admirable recovery from it. Although he had said that plain speaking was over for now, Maya well understood that he had an underlying message for her but, in no way an inept or obvious man, he soon moved on to other subjects. He asked about the research that John had been doing in Cambridge. He told them about the hospital where he worked and the enormous strides that still had to be made in India to give its population proper access to health care. Soshan talked about domestic matters and in describing her flat and telling them something about Mary, gave them some idea of how she had been living all these years. Maya avoiding the personal side of her job dwelt on the background to it and explained how she was getting to know local people through working with them.

Almost before they realised it, the meal was over and they went into the lounge for coffee. Sohrab, subtly but definitely in charge, led Maya and Soshan to a corner seating arrangement and sat with John at a slight distance from them where, freed for a while from their constant, discreet surveillance of the two highly strung women whom they regarded as their responsibility, they began a soft-voiced, more relaxed discussion.

Alone with her daughter, Soshan at first took refuge in pouring their coffees and getting milk and sugar requirements right. Then she steeled herself and turned to Maya. "About the wedding. It isn't going to be a religious ceremony. You have no idea of the difficulties that could possibly cause. Even in these modern times there are issues around the status of Parsi women with non-Parsi husbands. There are still ongoing cases in the courts where such women are trying to assert their right even to enter our temples. Priests have been sued for conducting religious rituals involving such women and their children. Identity, Maya! It is so important to everyone. It's a serious issue for you I know." She paused and risked putting out a hand, only to pull it back hastily when she saw Maya stiffen. "Darling, I was so young when I came to England with your father and started all this. You won't excuse me on those grounds because I was not so young when I left you and, like all children, you probably saw me as even older than I was. I believed that I loved your father. But I was certainly too young to realise that love and marriage aren't totally private matters. They involve other people. If I'd chosen a Parsi, I'd have been given a complete package. Love might or might not have been part of it, but there would have been a whole community that would have enclosed me and any children of mine, that would have given us a sense of belonging and protected us. In England I was on my own in a way that I had never experienced. The setting, the attitudes I encountered were alien to me and it often felt as if I were acting a part, within a stage set that I recognised from literature and films but that often felt strangely unreal."

"And you wanted to make me face that same thing!" Maya's face was red and her voice hoarse. "That's how I would have felt in India if you'd taken me there."

"I realise that now. But it's too late." She leaned forward and said urgently, "Please, Maya, let's forget it all and remember how incredibly, almost impossibly, lucky we are. Look over there. See those two wonderful men. Our second chance. Let's take it. Let's not allow what has happened between us, what has warped us both, to ruin it."

Maya looked over at John. He was the important person in her life. Her mother was right. It wasn't what had happened but what she allowed it to do to her that could harm him.

"It's not easy for me." She met her mother's pleading eyes, her own wide and serious. "But maybe if I try to behave as if there is no lingering pain in me, slowly, hopefully, in the end there won't be any. But you'll have to stay cool. Don't make a fuss or get emotional. Let's just be practical. Tell me more about what you are planning. You were saying that you couldn't have a religious ceremony."

Soshan letting out a relieved breath, sat back and said with only a slight tremor, "Yes, well as I said, there are continuing disputes over the status of women like me. Already a very small community, Parsis are facing declining numbers but they still have a strong incentive to keep their bloodlines pure." For a second she lost her intensity and gave a faint laugh. "That makes us sound as if we are racehorses. It can be seen as peculiar by outsiders but you have to understand how we fled Persia and Islam, all those years ago, to hold on to our religion, our customs and, once again we come back to it, our unique identity. We have managed to keep those intact for so long, it would be a tragedy for them to be lost now. Still, it raises serious issues for people like me. Even though I'm now marrying a good Parsi, by previously marrying and divorcing a foreigner I am left unsure of where I stand. But you don't want to hear all that. The fact is that we have decided to avoid any controversy and have a civil ceremony in your grandparents' flat with immediate family only and a party for friends at a hotel afterwards. I really want you to be there. It won't be the same without you and not an auspicious start for us."

"We'll come." Maya said curtly. "But as John so often says to me, 'We don't want a drama.' Let's take it one step at a time."

As they said goodnight, they were all fairly satisfied with the way things were going and less stressed than they would have believed possible earlier in the evening. Maya barely flinched when her mother hugged her. More importantly, she and John had agreed to go to India and Soshan had insisted that she would immediately book and pay for their flight and make all the necessary arrangements.

The following day, they were all glad to breakfast in their rooms, to postpone seeing each other until lunchtime, but even this delay was not enough for Maya and following John to the lift at noon, she came to an abrupt standstill, her whole body dragging at her. She did not want this. She had done enough.

"I forgot something. You go on and I'll come down in a few moments."

John turned back. "I'll wait for you. There is no rush."

"No, really." She decided to be open with him. "Please, John, go ahead. I actually need a few moments alone."

He hesitated, then gave way. "Right, but if you are too long I shall come for you."

Maya went back to their room and sat on the bed, wrapping her arms round her chest. She longed to be safely in Hadleigh, with time to think about the agreed trip to India. Last night this had seemed not only feasible but exciting. In the cooler light of morning, the full reality of it having hit her, it had been something that she must go through with. Now, at the prospect of seeing both her parents at the same time, in the same room, it was a potential nightmare. Her mother might well flaunt it in front of her father and the thought of again being a pawn between them made her feel sick and feverish. She stood up rather shakily. John would be waiting for her and if he came back there would have to be explanations that she did not feel up to. She went into the bathroom rinsed her face with cold water, redid her lipstick and went out to the lift.

Downstairs, she stood looking through a glass door and saw everyone standing near the long table that had been set for them at the end of the dining room. It was like watching a tableau of the key figures in her life.

Soshan had reverted to western dress this morning. This ambivalent attitude to identity had always struck Maya, determinedly intent on clarity about her own, as a flaw, but she had learned a great deal recently from some hastily undertaken reading and was more informed and less critical. On first arriving in India, the Parsis had accepted the wearing of Indian dress as one of the conditions imposed on them in return for the right to stay there and when they later became involved in a close co-operation with the British Raj, they adopted a more frequent use of European clothes. Dress, for them, was apparently an incidental and superficial issue. What counted was their survival as a community. They needed inner steadfastness not intransigence. Flexibility was a weapon. The relevance of these ideas to her own situation was not lost on Maya. In a small but similar way she too had been intent on survival but, far from flexible, had been impossibly intransigent. Here was another pointer to a better way of doing things.

She looked with a dawning admiration at her mother, standing undaunted between the two men in her life. If one were fanciful, they could be seen as her good and bad angels, the analogy weakened by the fact that virtue was dark-haired and dark-eyed, while blond hair and blue eyes had been deceptive and untrustworthy. Those blue eyes looked wary. Peter was obviously not prepared to concede anything to this newcomer or allow himself to be upstaged in any way. Her grandmother, in sober navy, and Karen, in a suede suit, cashmere jumper and uncomfortably high heels, were hovering, unnoticed, on the edge of this compelling, central trio. John was standing a little apart from them all.

"Excuse me. It's Maya isn't it?"

She turned to see a short, elderly woman in a white sari and heavy knitted jacket looking up at her with a broad smile. "You must be surprised to be accosted like this by a total stranger, but I shared a flight to India with your mother not so long ago. She talked about you and showed me your photograph. That's how I recognised you. I dare say that you know nothing about me. I'm Mariam Thomas." She nodded towards the group beyond the door, "I'm far from being a shrinking violet but one feels a little awkward walking into such a gathering alone. Perhaps you will, only metaphorically of course, hold my hand and take me in with you." She had seen the expression of near panic on Maya's face and had a shrewd idea that she too needed a hand to hang on to.

They went together to be jointly greeted by Peter and Soshan. After nerving herself up to this moment, Maya was unreasonably put out by their unemotional reception of her and thrown by their unexpectedly casual manner with each other. They were caught up in social duties, with several people to distract them. Peter, primarily intent on weighing up this other man in Soshan's life, gave Maya only fleeting attention and spoke distractedly about her new home and her new job. If he had been told of her prospective trip to India he did not mention it. He totally ignored Mariam after being introduced to her and Soshan, irritated by his cavalier attitude, turned to talk pointedly and animatedly to her friend. Karen, disregarded by Peter, had attached herself to her mother-in-law, the only other person she had any real connection with, and was fluttering her eyelashes at Sohrab who was being affable and polite to Mrs Fielding. He ignored her flirtatious manner and, as soon as possible without obvious rudeness, rejoined Soshan and Mariam. Peter, still with half his attention focussed on Sohrab, had begun a conversation with John. Maya went over to her grandmother.

"So my dear, Soshan tells me that you are going to her wedding. I can imagine how glad your Indian grandparents will be to see you."

"I doubt that they are interested in me. They may well be angry because I have not been in touch with them all these years. They have other, more amenable and satisfactory grandchildren."

"Well, I have only you and I am certainly a little angry with you but a grandchild is something special, however remote."

"Oh, Granny," Maya moved closer to her, "I'm sorry. I know that I have treated you shabbily. After lunch we'll sit down together and make those arrangements for you to stay with us."

Before she could say any more, they were all called to find their seats at the table and choose their food. As they sat down, she looked regretfully across at John, who was placed opposite her, wishing that she could share her subversive thoughts with him. It was quite deflating to think that, even keyed up to emotional heights, people were quickly and easily diverted by wholly mundane activities and genetically programmed to put masticating and digesting food very high on a list of survival priorities. It cast a harsh light on all their many pretensions and made it a little ridiculous, as her mother would no doubt have phrased it, to be high-flown and intense about life.

With lunch over and coffee put ready for them in the lounge they divided into congenial groups. Sohrab sat with Mariam deep in a conversation about shared professional interests and Maya pulled a chair closer to her grandmother with a firm intention of completing their plans for her to come to Hadleigh. Peter, Soshan and John were carrying on a heated discussion of British aid to India, a topic that they had started over dessert and on which they all held strong opinions. Karen sat with them, the fixed smile on her face that of someone feigning interest in ideas completely beyond comprehension. Soshan, noticing her discomfort, stood up pushing back her chair and said, "You men carry on. I'm going to talk to Karen. We have a lot to tell each other about organising a big event. She can give me some advice. Let's sit over here, Karen, where we can be private."

Peter glanced up at her briefly but was soon re-launched on the argument he had been propounding and even John, preparing to make a point, hardly noticed her gesture.

"She is a good person, your mother." Her grandmother, while listening to Maya, had kept an eye on everyone and had noticed it. "I'm sorry things worked out so badly between us. However, she is doing the right thing now. This Sohrab is a perfect choice. I know you think I am bigoted but I'm merely old-fashioned. I believe that a shared background is a solid foundation for a marriage. That's not racist. I could prove that by saying what I think about your father's new wife but I'll not meddle again. It's not helpful."

Maya felt suddenly weary. She wanted to hear no more of these overtones and layers of resentment, guilt and blame, all this wariness and introspection, these endless retrials.

"Excuse me, Granny. Just have to go to the cloakroom. I'll be back in a moment."

She stood at the washbasin and ran cold water over her wrists and wiped her forehead with a damp paper towel. As she pulled out a second one, the door opened and Mariam came in.

"Oh you are here, Maya! Are you all right, my dear?"

"Yes, I'm fine. The whole family thing was just a bit overwhelming for a moment and I needed a break from it all."

"I can see that with the situation between your parents, you might feel a little under strain. I must say, though, that I am full of admiration for your mother. She is behaving well in trying circumstances." She gave Maya a long look. "You probably wonder what right I have to an opinion. Soshan and I seem to be no more than acquaintances, our only connection a shared a flight to India, but there was something about our common experience of England that drew us together and we have stayed in touch and shared a lot of confidences."

"Do you think we could find a quiet spot to sit and talk for a few minutes before we go back inside?" Maya was struck by the thought that this dumpy little woman with the plain face might have things to tell her that would be interesting and useful.

After they had found two corner chairs in a small lounge, however, she fidgeted for a while as if unable to get comfortable.

"How long have you lived in England, Dr Thomas?"

"Oh please, dear, call me Mariam. I've been here most of my adult life. I was a green girl when I arrived and now I am a weathered and gnarled old woman. Not as weathered as I might have been. If I'd lived in India, I'd have been shrivelled by heat and sun by now but I've stayed plump, bulky even, preserved by the cold." She gave Maya a wicked grin. "There are always plus as well as minus points to every choice we make."

"Has my mother talked to you about the choice that she made?" Maya looked diffident, slightly ashamed of such needy curiosity.

"Not perhaps as much as you are hoping." Mariam's eyes were kind and shrewd. "Enough to make me aware of the tensions between you, enough to know why she did what she did and make it understandable to me, but enough also to make me feel deeply for what it must have done to you. Still, I begin to see a happy ending to all this. You have both found good men to share your lives with. I am essentially a solitary creature for whom work has taken the place of such human ties. I try to think that I have lived a worthwhile life but I have some regrets about the things I've missed out on. It's best to avoid pointless heart-searching but in some ways, I do envy you."

"Do you have any family, Mariam?" Maya was diverted from her own preoccupations and pierced with a sudden realisation of how lonely some lives could be.

"I do have nieces and nephews in South India and they always welcome me back warmly. I am invited for special occasions; their marriages, the births of their children," her eyes gleamed mischievously, "funerals even. But we live very separate, very separated lives. I have become a sort of hybrid who no longer fits totally into the old patterns." She looked across the room, lost in thought and then pulled her attention back to Maya. "But we shouldn't make too much of this split personality dilemma. Nowadays everyone is more individualistic, egocentric even, hooked on selfies and defining themselves less and less by any sort of group identity." Again she seemed to drift off into her own thoughts before saying briskly, "I try to remember that there are huge advantages in a wider experience, a broader outlook that can outweigh the disadvantages of dislocation. We come back to the question of choice. This is what I chose, wisely or not. It has to be lived with. I'm sorry that in your case another person's choice had such an effect on your life but you look to me like someone who will live with that too. Enough though. Given half a chance, I climb onto a soapbox. I'll climb down. We'd better rejoin the others."

"Mariam, I'd like to see you again. Maybe you could come to Norfolk sometime." Maya, like her mother, was instantly taken by this plain-spoken little woman.

"I'd like that. My contact with your mother is regrettably long distance. It would be good to see you again as another way of keeping in touch with her; to keep in touch with you in your own right, let me hasten to add. If you ever come to London, call me."

They returned a little regretfully to the party, which finally ended at around four. Mariam had ordered a taxi and the announcement by a waiter that this had arrived was the signal for a general exodus.

Peter, shepherding his women to the car, was waved off by Soshan and Sohrab, while John and Maya sat on in the lounge and gave one another tired smiles. By common consent all four survivors decided that they should spend the evening apart and only meet for breakfast and lunch the next day before John and Maya left for Norfolk.

As they drove off in the early afternoon, Maya fastened her seat belt with relief. After all her agonising, the weekend had not been quite the ordeal that she had dreaded but she was glad that it was safely over. Being examined by Sohrab's clinical eye had been disconcerting and a little humiliating even though she recognised that his straightforward manner had actually made it easier for them. That clear-sighted, unsentimental attitude may well have influenced and steadied her mother. Both her parents would inevitably change because of the new partners they had chosen. It had been an odd experience seeing them together in the same space but no longer an entity. The image of that entity, so long burned into her imagination with all its baleful side effects, had suddenly lost a great deal of its power.

The hurdles of the lunch party had been safely negotiated and if India, a far bigger hurdle, still loomed over her, she was almost ready for it. She looked across at John and her throat tightened. They would get through this. It could even turn out to be a positive adventure. Neither of them had enjoyed the freedom and frivolity of many of their contemporaries. Neither of them had taken a gap year. Her earlier time in Bombay as a five year old had an insubstantial, dreamlike quality and this would be a first for both of them. If she had earlier admitted to viewing their life as the Maya and John story, this would open a quite different chapter in that joint biography, introducing new backgrounds and characters to expand and broaden it.

She looked out at the frantic traffic around them, mentally slapping herself down, 'What was that you thought about being less high-flown only a short while ago?' She was glad that she hadn't shared what her mother might well have described as these ridiculous fancies with John. Reality was enough to be going on with.

EIGHTEEN

If January had been moody and changeable, ending with a final spectacular display of Christmas card landscapes, February, despite a sharp wind that never really died away, was consistently sunny. Maya, who had not been into the garden for almost two months, was tempted by this illusion of spring into venturing out and opening the gate onto the meadow. The trees were skeletal and the reeds and grasses dry and brown but, lit by the pale sunshine, had an austere beauty. She caught intermittent flashes of the stream, a few birds flitting above it and, to her delight, saw the owl make three swift, low passes over the ground before melting into the grey-brown distance. Within a few minutes, though, the wind erased any idea of sitting here hoping to see it again and she retreated to her room, an alternative comfort zone.

It had already become a place where life could be put on hold. Her nerves alternately vibrating to echoes of the events in London and taut in anticipation of the coming journey to India, it was taking time to get back into the slow routines of farmhouse and schoolwork. In here, she was learning to lose herself in books, to sit flooding and transforming any troubled silence with music or merely to dream while gazing out of the window into the wilder garden beyond. John and Robert rarely came in and never sat with her but had demonstrated interest and approval by making contributions of various kinds. John had bought her a sound system and, out of the blue, Robert had turned up after a day in Norwich with a gift; a painting of the Norfolk countryside, a slightly abstract representation of it, in the soft greens and browns reminiscent of her favourite view.

"Robert! It's beautiful. Thank you." She had been so delighted, not only with the picture itself but this gesture of thoughtfulness, that she had kissed him warmly on the cheek.

"Ah, well!" He looked awkward but gratified. "That's not a great thing, not a masterpiece, I daresay, but I thought you'd like it."

Joyce, when she next came, stared up in astonishment to where it hung above the bureau.

"That is progress. For Robert to buy a present under his own steam for anyone is a wonder in itself, that he has bought one for you and one so totally right... I'm lost for words."

Whenever she came to the farm, the two of them shared time here and, if they always had plenty to talk about, there were now momentous developments to discuss.

"It sounds like a long time but it's only six weeks before our flight. You will be left to nursemaid Robert again." Maya studied Joyce thoughtfully. "You get all the bad deals and you are so patient. I wish that you could come with us. Would you like to see India?"

"In a way, yes. If there was a magic carpet or flying was the elegant, leisurely business it used to be, maybe, but with airports the way they are and the world the way it is, I think even staying with Robert may be less traumatic. I'm a bit set in my ways, perhaps, to take on all that turmoil. What I hope is that your mother will come here, so that if I never see her country, at least I do get a chance to see her."

"I have made up my mind to invite her. I promise. Before too long. And Sohrab, of course. I think you will like him, Joyce. Somehow seeing them as a couple has changed the way I feel in an extraordinary way. They may be here this summer. Meanwhile, my granny is coming. She called to say that she can't make it as soon as we'd planned as she has gone down with some horrible, viral thing and has to wait till that clears up, but we've persuaded her that she could at least recuperate here. It is a bit wintry but she doesn't want to gad about much. By the time she comes, anyway, it will be almost the middle of March and it could be slightly warmer. John hopes to fetch her in about a week's time and she can stay until just before we leave."

When she did finally arrive, Maya was shocked by how frail and old her grandmother looked but, warmly welcomed by Robert, who saw her as being very much like Iva in her spirited determination not to be defeated by age, and pampered by Mrs Hemsby, who possibly saw the same similarities, she soon regained strength and colour. She and Joyce immediately got on well, were soon on first name terms and while Maya was at work and John and his uncle were out and about on the farm, spent several mornings together.

"This place has proved perfect for Maya, Joyce. Your son is such a good influence on her. I can't tell you how relieved I am that she has the family she always wanted. Poor child. She had such a bad start."

"Mrs Fielding, sorry Nora, I'm going to be horribly, perhaps unforgivably, frank." Joyce ran her fingers through her hair as if straightening something inside her head. "Maya and I had a bad start too. I admit to thinking that she was wrong for John." She put out a restraining hand. "No. Let me finish. The fact that Maya herself was hostile towards her mother obviously didn't prevent her from resenting what she saw as your prejudice against her. I just want to say that I understand exactly what it is like to see a son marry someone unsuitable."

"Well my dear, I did feel as you did. I don't deny it. Maya is mistaken, though, in believing that I blame Soshan entirely for all that went wrong. We saw photographs of her at home in which she was always surrounded by smiling people; parents, sisters, cousins, servants. It must have been difficult to find herself so often alone and, when alone with a small baby, without the kind of support that she had always been used to, it was probably quite daunting. She only had me and I wasn't exactly what she would have asked for. Peter left her to it and was, in my opinion, as much, if not more, at fault." She shook her head impatiently. "Well, I wasn't as understanding then either. I had a lot to learn." She gave Joyce a rather wistful look. "Like me, you must have found that widowhood teaches you a great deal. You find out what it's like to lose someone you have always taken for granted and how hard it can be to have no-one to lean on. Still, for a long time, turned in on yourself, you see this as your own unique suffering. Growing old changes one. At my age friends are departing at an accelerating rate and life is increasingly lonely. Alarming too! Every illness is a warning signal! That gives you perspective. I have long realised that Soshan has more basic sense than Peter. What about this new wife of his?" She and Joyce exchanged a meaningful look. "I thought at first that he seemed to be set on making another mistake but this one might just work out for him. I would say that there are few illusions on either side this time around to cause problems."

Soon after their conversation, Peter, blissfully oblivious to these criticisms, to any possibility that he might be criticised, descended on Hadleigh for a second time, having called to ask if he could come for the day while his mother was with them. Maya had spoken to him and said rather brusquely that it would be fine.

"Karen won't be coming. She has some girly weekend set up with friends. In any case the countryside is not really her thing."

Maya picked up this rather mocking mimicry and was on the point of giving him a sharp reprimand before deciding to ignore it. She had no intention of colluding with him in any denigration of his new wife and was irritated by his obvious attempt to imply some special bond, some secret from her that they could share. She had a momentary recollection of Soshan rescuing Karen from social unease and taking her off for a chat at their London lunch. It was not right to be soft on him simply because she expected less of him and she was very short with him.

The day passed off surprisingly well. Though he spent much of his time with Robert and John, Peter did sit with his mother for quite a while. Maya told herself, with some cynicism, that he realised that she was getting kindlier treatment here than he and Karen usually offered her and was, as always, unwilling to be outdone in any arena but, whatever the motive, his attention brought a welcome sparkle to her grandmother's eyes. He was totally at ease with them all and, appearing to be in no hurry to leave, accepted a last-minute invitation to share supper with them, so it was not until they were alone in their room at the end of the day that Maya and John were able to talk about him.

"He's still not mentioned our Indian trip or the reason for it. In fact," Maya looked at John thoughtfully, "I don't think he mentioned Mother or Sohrab once today. How odd is that?"

"Well, he can be odd, or perhaps I should say aloof, where people are concerned. He's a 'business first' man. It's the way he is." John sounded untroubled. "He was really into my rental plans and has promised to put the word out among colleagues and friends as soon as we are up and running. I told him that with all that has happened this year, I'm setting a deadline for late summer next year. I must say it's encouraging to get his endorsement."

Maya climbed into bed and pulled the covers high round her chin. "Even you are a 'business first' man then, John. I'm glad he will be of use to you."

John got in beside her. "I wouldn't say first. Business is important but it's not the main thing on my mind at this moment. I'm not at all aloof where people are concerned."

The next day, they began to get things ready for their journey. Time away was limited by the demands of Maya's new job and as she had decided to wear the same outfit for this wedding as for Peter's and had an adequate supply of summery clothes, there was not much to do on the shopping or packing front. Her grandmother had to be taken home, though, and they were just making plans for John to drive her there two days before they were due to leave when Joyce intervened.

"Maya, do you think your grandmother would like to stay on while you are away. She is going back to an empty house and I will be here alone with Robert. The two of them get on unexpectedly well and I would really appreciate the company. You could take her back after you return. You are only going for two weeks, after all, and you could tell her about it and show her any photographs you have taken before she leaves."

This was an arrangement that suited, indeed delighted, everyone. Robert was glad of someone with whom to share convivial evenings that would otherwise, shut in with Joyce, become far less cheerful. She felt exactly the same about sharing them with him. Nora, as she had now become to them both, looked forward to such evenings as a pleasure that would be sadly missed when she was on her own again. John was relieved of a long drive to Berkshire prior to a tiring flight and Maya knew that she would leave with an easy mind, thinking of her grandmother cosy and cared for in this comfortable old house. There seemed to be something about it, its age, its solidity that was slowly drawing in her rather forlorn, unloving family around her and giving her the novel feeling of being the at the heart of it.

Somewhat overwrought at the thought of the venture ahead of her she had, in her mind's eye, an imaginary companion piece for Robert's landscape; an interior, warm and golden, with seated figures round a blazing fire. This offset any vision of sun and heat or exotic, oriental scenes, as she and John waved them all goodbye and set off for the airport through the early chill of a windy March morning.

NINETEEN

Their plane landed just before midnight, so that all Maya saw, peering out into the night as they descended, was darkness spangled with lights. Even in daylight, however, her view would have been, in a unique way, unrevealing. Not so long ago, world travellers, looking out of their aircraft windows, would have immediately known in which city they were about to land by the distinctive architecture below them. Now, all larger cities, whether in the West or the East, are beginning to take on a generic, cosmopolitan appearance. Having horribly polluted this pleasant, green planet, people seem to feel an increasing urge to escape from it, to send up slender constructions of steel and glass, high into emptiness, high above the corrupted canyons below them, as if on the first step of a journey into space that will allow them to escape the consequences of their careless folly. The inside rooms of these modern buildings are then left exposed to the outside as if to exclude any possibility of hiding what might be done there in the future, cutting off any retreat into the secrecy of bricks and mortar.

Bombay, a large metropolis clinging to a small land mass, has always been a city between sea and sky, its upward surge inevitable. It is also a city between splendour and squalor, wealth and want, hope and despair, industry and indolence, aspiration and apathy, originality and orthodoxy, trendiness and tradition. On its frenetic roads, luxury limousines glide through volatile battalions of taxis, scooters, rickshaws and handcarts. Its tower blocks and skyscrapers soar above ageless bazaars, ancient temples, dhobi ghats and imposing public buildings that were aliens, too, in their time, thrusting Victorian energy and effervescence out into languid oriental surroundings. Its population includes people occupying the equivalent of Trump Tower and people whose home could be a cloth tied to a fence in simulation of a tent. To have only two weeks to explore this place was like having three minutes to read the Encyclopaedia Britannica.

Soshan came alone to meet them, using the lateness of the hour as an excuse for any lack of a large, enthusiastic reception committee such as those they saw all around them. Maya and John were whisked through the airport building, allowed the briefest inhalation of the pungent, humid air outside before being installed in, if not a limousine, a large air-conditioned car and driven along less frantic, night-time roads by a uniformed driver.

"You will be tired," Soshan was authoritative. "No matter what is done to make a flight bearable, nearly ten hours is a long time to be shut up in a tube filled with stale air, eating less than gourmet food. You were sensible to take a non-stop flight but that also limits your options. No chance of even short escapes. Now! You are coming to my flat where you are to stay, looked after by my Mary. I'm moving up to your grandparents' place, Maya. Having my small flat to yourselves will be more comfortable than being plunged into their larger but busier one. You aren't used to the lack of privacy and the constant commotion caused by servants all over the place. As it's only upstairs, I don't have to make a major transfer of my belongings. In effect, I shall simply be sleeping there. I'll have my meals with you."

"We are putting you to some trouble though." John looked doubtful.

"I don't even know the meaning of that word right now. If you only knew how thrilled I am that you are here." She was doing her best to be as cool as Maya had asked her to be and to avoid any provocative action or remark but could not stop herself from blurting out, "If only you could stay longer."

"I explained that." Maya was instantly on the defensive at the slightest hint of criticism. "With such a new job, I didn't want to ask for favours or any extra time off and the Easter break is short. We've come and we'll share your big day. Leaving immediately afterwards seems to me sensible timing. You and Sohrab won't want to nursemaid us but to have time to yourselves. Are you going away anywhere?"

"We're spending a few days alone together at a hill station not far from here. In our situation any talk of a honeymoon would be ridiculous. Our plan is to wait and combine a longer holiday with a trip to Europe at the end of July when Sohrab has some conference to attend in Frankfurt." She gave Maya a fleeting look. "Hopefully we can get together then, but we'll discuss all that later. Let's settle you in, get you some light food and then you can shower and sleep. We can talk over breakfast."

As the car drew up to a flight of stone steps with a dim light at the top of it, their first, shadowy impression was of a low, chunky building dwarfed by the pale outlines of towering, intimidating neighbours. The flat was on the third of four floors and reached by means of a small, creaky lift.

"This is quite an old structure and parts of it need constant attention." Soshan clanged the door firmly shut. "My parents have lived here since before I was born. These old places are receding into history and we are lucky that we have stopped it being torn down to make space for a modern monster. We still enjoy a very human, friendly atmosphere. There are only five flats, one on each floor, with two smaller converted ones on my floor."

Her flat might be considered small in the sense that it had few rooms but standing in the square, tiled hall looking round, the three that they could see into, a study, a bedroom and a living room, all looked very spacious. Before they could make any further move, a small woman in a white sari emerged from a passage at the side and stood with bowed head, hands joined in a traditional Indian greeting.

"John, Maya, meet Mary." Soshan was faintly smiling, her tone amused. "This docile appearance is not to be taken at face value. She is actually a very spunky Christian and by tomorrow, she will have discarded this Hindu-style meekness and, all too soon, be telling you what is what."

Mary looked up at her reproachfully and turned to Maya. "It is very good you come to see your mother. She is always very sad without you."

"See! She is already climbing onto a hobby horse. Come through here." Soshan, with a backward glare and giving them no time to do more than smile at Mary, hastily led them into the bedroom and showed them the bathroom that led off it. "I'll leave you to freshen up. Come through to the living room when you're ready."

"Well, here we are at last. I didn't ever think to see you in India. I'm proud of you Maya." John closed the door behind them and tried to take her in his arms, but gazing round she had caught sight of all the photographs on the chest of drawers and did not respond.

"Look at those. Nothing but me. Do you think that is deliberate, a mini propaganda ploy?"

"No, I do not. They look very much part of the fixtures and fittings. Don't spoil things by being all prickly and suspicious."

"Sorry. Actually, I'm quite excited now that I'm here though we shan't have time to see all that much. I won't be able to compete with the women at school."

"If you want to see more, we can always come again. It all sounds very hopeful to me. Now, I'm not really hungry but obviously food has been prepared for us and we need to eat something."

After they had eaten and the table had been cleared, Mary retreated into her room and Soshan prepared to go upstairs. "I've asked Mary not to bring tea in to you in the morning. I thought you'd find that intrusive. When you wake up, give her a call and she'll bring it out to you on the balcony. It's quite cool outside early in the morning. We'll breakfast there together when I come down, before making plans for the day." Soshan gave John an unapologetic kiss, made a slightly diffident movement of her lips close to Maya's cheek and left them.

They slept soundly in the darkened room, the unfamiliar but soothing drone of an air-conditioner like a modern lullaby. Stepping out onto the balcony the next morning, the combined heat and noise hit them like a physical blow. If background noises could be compared to music, the sounds of Norfolk might be characterised as a gentle and melodic folk tune while here, the effect was that of one of the more avant-garde, discordant pieces by a modern composer. If this was the song of India it was being sung *forte* and *con brio*.

Over breakfast with Soshan, distracted by the scenes of domestic life being played out uninhibitedly on neighbouring balconies like some exotic soap opera with an insistent backing theme, it was hard to attend to what she was saying, but it was, nevertheless, apparent to them that any plans for the day had already been fixed. Their opinions were not needed.

"As soon as we've eaten I am taking you on a non-stop, overview car tour. We'll take in some of the main tourist sites later but this will give you an immediate and general impression of the city. We're having lunch upstairs with your grandparents and we'll take a rest, maybe even a short sleep, in the afternoon." Soshan caught Maya's dubious expression. "You will be glad of it, I promise. The climate is reasonable at the moment but a big change from what you are used to and the humidity can be tiring. Besides, at seven we're going over to Sohrab's flat for dinner and you will meet his daughters. They eat very late so it will be a long and possibly emotionally draining day."

This seemed likely to be true and, though they remained seated in the air-conditioned comfort of the car, the incessant movement of traffic and crowds around them and the scale and novelty of what they were being asked to take in made their morning tour surprisingly exhausting. It was made more so for Maya by an equally incessant internal buzz of thoughts and images that matched the kaleidoscopic parade outside. She only half heard Soshan's on-going commentary, catching the odd word here and there – Haji Ali, Victoria Station, Gateway of India, Prince of Wales Museum – but failing to really register the buildings in question. It was all a bit of a blur. Caught up in her personal drama, it was impossible to act the part of a tourist. She was intensely nervous about the coming meeting with her grandparents who would hardly be delighted to see her. She had no idea of how she could or should behave.

It was not as bad as she had anticipated. Used to every shade of social demand or family contretemps, her grandparents were too experienced and sophisticated to display discomfort even supposing that they felt any. Their well-honed skills, John's presence and the need for them to get to know him carried them through the initial moments and kept them going as they went in for lunch. Maya, not so much relieved at escaping any prolonged scrutiny as irrationally dismayed at being sidelined by their interest in her new husband, did feel uncomfortably mean and petty. Then she got a share of the attention.

"Come, my dear," – her grandmother led her to a seat at a large, polished table in the dining room that aroused vague memories in her – "you did not enjoy our food all those years ago. You were very young, of course, and your tastes must have changed but I have made sure that we have plenty of mild and un-spiced dishes for you."

This was her only reference to the past and, with her grandfather clearly more interested in John and soon deeply involved in a conversation with him about his research and current work on the farm, Maya found herself carried along in the wake of her grandmother and her mother, both voluble and assertive women with many details of the coming ceremony still to discuss and last minute decisions still to make about Soshan's programme for their entertainment. The immediate concern was the large, family dinner party on the following evening at which Maya and John would meet her aunts and cousins and this was gone over at length. Her earlier dismay slowly gave way to a half-relieved gratitude for the speed with which she had been subsumed into their concerns, all emotional traumas apparently to be ignored. It was rather comforting to be less important to them than she had supposed herself to be.

She was more grateful than she had expected for the siesta that Soshan had decreed and got up, after an actual sleep, to bath and dress for an evening which had its own likely pitfalls. No amount of salutary reminders of her relative unimportance could silence her clamorous thoughts about coming face to face with Sohrab's daughters. She was conscious of conflicting forces driving her; an undeniable jealousy at the thought of their future role in Soshan's life and a horrified pity for all that they must have undergone in losing their mother. This was going to be another testing encounter.

"I'm looking forward to seeing Sohrab again. He is very much my kind of person and your mother is very lucky to have him." John, who had rested only briefly and quietly dressed while she was sleeping, stood in the bedroom doorway as she began to make up her face and do her hair.

He watched her applying eye-shadow. "Have you ever used that stuff before? You seem to be taking a lot of trouble. You aren't worried about this evening are you?" He came up behind her and put his arms round her.

"John, I'll smudge this. Be careful. And mind my hair."

"No, let's not be careful. There's no need, Maya. Everything is going well. Everything is going to be fine. *You* are doing well and you are also going to be fine. Just relax and enjoy yourself. And you don't need all that make-up. You are beautiful enough."

"Well, it's a kind of armour really, so indulge me. I've finished anyway. I'm ready."

Sohrab lived on the top floor of a long-established but modern-looking block of flats on the seashore. A white-clad servant was waiting for them as they came out of the lift and took them from the hall, through a long drawing room and out onto a wide, softly-lit balcony where he and his daughters were waiting. Even this early in the evening the natural light had almost faded, but the last rays of the vanishing sun were creating a narrow pathway across the darkened sea beyond the balustrade.

"The view at the moment is a bit pop art but it is quite spectacular by day." Sohrab smiled at Soshan, shook hands with John and then, with a questioning look, brushed Maya's cheek with a passing touch of lips. "We don't have the atmosphere of an old building but we have the sea and it's very pleasant to be able to look out and think there is nothing between us and Arabia. Such space, such vastness is a consoling concept after spending the day in the crowded city. It can be a bit troublesome here during the monsoon because we are very exposed, but that is a price worth paying."

This chatty manner, uncharacteristically unfocussed, made Maya wonder fleetingly if he might be nervous. Then he regained his usual self- command.

"There are no other guests tonight. This is our chance to get to know each other better. John, Maya, here are my daughters." He put an arm around the smaller, plumper of the two girls who had come forward with him and dropped a swift kiss on the top of her short, curly hair. "This little one, Persis, is surprisingly the older of the two. I can tell you that what she lacks in inches she makes up for in spirit." He reached out to draw the second girl closer, "And this is Kerman. She just keeps growing and is, as you see, already almost as tall as me."

The two girls were very different, not only in height but in every way, and would hardly have been taken for sisters. Persis was darker, with a round, cheerful face, a small pert nose and dimples. Kerman was slender and fairer, her face thinner and more serious and her straight hair drawn back into a severe knot. Standing next to her father, her resemblance to him was marked.

"Maya, at last. We've been so longing to see you." Persis spoke rapidly, in a light, high voice. "We're thrilled that you have come for the wedding. You are, after all, a new sister."

"We heard a lot about you from Daddy, after he met you in London. We are pleased to meet you. And you too John." Kerman spoke slowly and in deeper tones. Her eyes were slightly guarded.

Maya had seen each of them give Soshan a quick hug but they had as yet not spoken to her. She wondered how they truly felt. Their closeness to their father and his deep affection for them were obvious and anyone coming into that united circle would inevitably be something of an intruder. She was surprised to feel a slight pang on behalf of her mother and was, ironically, anxious that these two girls should treat her kindly.

202

Sohrab invited them to help themselves from a selection of snacks and drinks set out on a side table and then either by design or accident, sat down near Soshan, leaving John and Maya slightly apart with the two girls. In the hour before dinner, they heard all about the course that Persis was doing, Kerman's hopes for a good result at the end of her final school year and her plan to follow her father into medicine and to train in England if possible.

By the end of the evening the girls were totally relaxed with John but perhaps a little less so with Maya. She could see that it might well be her own reserve that was to blame and, to signal a willingness to be friendly, agreed to meet them the following afternoon for an outing to the centre of the city. They planned to start off at a gallery where there was an exhibition of student art in which Persis had some textiles on display, to go on to some shops to look at shoes, saris and handbags and to finish with tea at the Taj Mahal hotel.

"Just you, Maya." Persis looked apologetically at John. "We want it to be a girly afternoon. You must see what great fashion we have on offer here. We'll take John with us another time to somewhere more serious."

"That's fine," John grinned at her, "I'd like to see your exhibition but not at the cost of trailing round shops. I normally only shop about once a year and only then if it's really necessary."

The whole of the following day had, in fact, once more been meticulously planned. Sohrab wanted them to begin by seeing the hospital and some laboratories where he worked. These were felt to be of special interest to John. Soshan would join them and if the men got too caught up in these technical areas, she could take Maya off to see something more general. They arranged to set off sometime after breakfast the next morning.

At nine-thirty, John, keen to go off on this projected inspection tour, came out of the bedroom to find Maya still sitting on the balcony in her dressing gown looking a little limp and tired.

"John, can you go without me? I don't want to opt out of my afternoon with Kerman and Persis but I don't feel up to two expeditions in one day. I'd like to catch my breath a little and just sit here quietly by myself for a while."

Still on the alert for any sign of trouble with her health after his recent scare, John was only too ready for her to do as she asked. Soshan, when she came back from upstairs, was less prepared to leave her behind but the thought of her spending time with Sohrab's girls was so encouraging that she was willing to compromise.

"Perhaps we are rushing you a bit. We shall have lunch out so I'll tell Mary to get you something light. The girls will probably have taken you off before we get back so we'll see you again for the party this evening."

After they had left, Maya fetched a book that she had brought from home and tried to settle down with it but was constantly distracted by the activities on the opposite balconies. Tense and apprehensive about all that was happening to her so quickly it was, in any case, impossible to concentrate on reading and, when Mary came to ask her if she'd like coffee, she was glad of company to keep her from her thoughts.

"I don't want anything to drink, Mary. I would like someone to talk to. Stay and sit down.

"Have work to do and your lunch to get." Mary had a fleeting memory of a sickly, disappointing child in mind as she looked at this adult daughter who had caused Soshan so much grief and her manner was still uptight and unfriendly.

"Well just talk to me for a while. Tell me about yourself. I know that you came here from South India when you were quite young but I don't know anything about your family. Tell me about them."

"Sahib, Memsahib and Soshan bai my family." Mary's voice was unyielding. "Mother and father very old when I come here. Died very soon. I am youngest of eight children. Now only two sisters left. I don't go back. Not going back to my village for many years."

"Mary, I'm so sorry. It must be hard for you." Maya was horrified and could not really find adequate words to respond to this harsh picture.

"Not hard," Mary snapped. "I am lucky. Life too hard before. Here I have good place. Memsahib and Soshan bai always kind. I know your mother since she was small child." She shot Maya a defiant look. "I am too much pleased when she is back in India and I come to live with her. Take care of her." She turned to go, unsmiling and un-softened by friendly overtures. "Now I finish my work and get lunch ready."

Maya, who knew only too well how prickly she had been when defending her own identity all these years, understood Mary's refusal to accept sympathy, her refusal to give in to any depiction of her life that differed from her chosen version of it. Yet the idea of such hardship, for whatever Mary insisted on, hardship it had clearly been, saddened her. It was upsetting, mortifying even, to think about her own unrelenting preoccupation with her lesser trials. Yet it was important not to be either too high-minded or too hard on herself. The misery of one person does not negate that of another. She had suffered in her own way and been entitled to feel her own pain. The important thing was to get it into perspective and to put it behind her.

She gave up on her book, deciding that activity was the best antidote to all this introspection and there was plenty of that ahead of her. After her time with the girls, there were all her unknown aunts and cousins to face at yet another dinner. She thought longingly of the slow, quiet days at the farm and with a small sigh went in to dress for a hot afternoon in the city.

TWENTY

The gallery turned out to be old, thick-walled, high-ceilinged and cool. An hour there among the displays set up by the many art colleges and schools involved was both comfortable and stimulating and passed surprisingly quickly. Persis had contributed three lengths of fabric and several drawings to her group's stand.

"She is extremely talented." Maya turned to Kerman as Persis left them for a moment to talk to another student. "These are really striking designs."

"She gets that from our mother." Kerman's expression was non-committal but her voice was sad. "She was also an art student before she married our father. She encouraged us both to draw and paint when we were small and used to...." she broke off as her sister returned.

"So, Maya," Persis said gaily, her small face glowing with satisfaction, "you can see what great things we can do in this country. We have centuries of artistic excellence behind us. Now, I want to take you to a special Craft Emporium, then to some outlets for leather goods and finally to one of my favourite sari shops so you can see that this training isn't academic in any way. It all translates into serious commercial value."

The hour spent in the gallery was no preparation for the humid heat and crush of the streets beyond it that they stepped out into. They did have the car but they had to walk considerable distances between any convenient parking and the places that the girls wanted her to see. Accustomed merely to cursory purchases in the relatively sedate centre of Cambridge, Maya was confirmed in her opinion that shopping was not really for her. She tried to look as if she were enjoying it all but it was a relief to reach their final destination.

"What are you wearing to the wedding?" Persis looked around the lavish shelves and dazzling materials on display. "Something simple will be best for the morning ceremony but why don't you wear a sari for the party in the evening? That would be a marvellous surprise for your grandparents and Soshan. See how gorgeous these are. If we choose one for you right now there is still time to get a matching blouse made. Our tailor is a treasure when there is a panic on. Please say that you will."

"I couldn't. I don't know how to wear one. I'd look as though I were wearing fancy dress. It wouldn't feel right."

Maya's whole body was clenched in a passionate rejection of this idea but Persis, though so agreeable and light-hearted, could be very forceful.

"Nonsense, you would look fabulous and we can teach you how to put it on." For a fleeting moment she looked almost hostile. "Don't consider yourself only. This would be a perfect way to please your mother and do something special for her."

Kerman put a warning hand on her arm. "Persis, it's not for us to decide what Maya wears. I'm sure she has thought carefully about that and brought a special dress with her. Stop telling people what to do. You can be a little bully sometimes."

Persis leaned in towards her sister, speaking softly in Gujarati. Maya could barely catch and could not, in any case, understand what she was saying but was badly thrown by the strong undercurrent of emotion that was evident in both her tone and her expression.

"Better not to talk like that." Kerman also spoke in an undertone but in English. "You should be careful, Persis. Things are never as straightforward as you'd like them to be." She turned to Maya, "I'm sorry. It was rude to speak in a language that you can't understand but sometimes Persis gets carried away by her enthusiasms."

Maya, seeing their strained faces and the obvious tension between them, was struck by a blinding realisation of just how momentous this wedding must be for them. It was an inescapable finality, the day when their mother would be replaced by someone else in a very public ceremonial. Every small detail involved must be of huge importance for them. Conscious of how little thought she had given to what to wear for it and what that said about her own attitude, she was pierced by a hot shame.

"I'm sorry. I have some very childish hang-ups and should be less dogmatic." She gave a small, apologetic shrug and her mouth twisted. "I'm not really a great one for fashion and I can be very careless about my clothes but I will buy a sari and if you show me how, I'll try it on. I can't promise to wear it. I might be very uncomfortable in it."

Persis was instantly back to her former self and gave her a warm hug. "Oh, thank you. That's wonderful. Look, let's forget the hotel. We'll choose your sari and go straight home so that you can try it out." She shook her head impatiently, "No, we won't go to our place. Better if we come to Soshan's flat because you have to go on to your grandmother's dinner later and that will give us more time. Mary will make tea. We can borrow one of your mother's petticoats and manage without a blouse for now. We'll make do with a T shirt. You can practice walking. That might be hard at first. But I'm sure you'll soon get used to it and you will look lovely."

Kerman raised her eyebrows but, glad to see Persis herself again, went along with this plan and they drove back to the flat, where Mary greeted them with the news that John had gone out with Soshan on some new errand. They would be back at around six.

"Bring us tea, Mary." Maya saw that Persis was quite at home, must have been here often and, to judge by Mary's broad smile, was very much a favourite. "Then, my dear, you have to leave us. We are planning a secret. When Soshan bai gets here, give us a minute's warning and I'll fetch her to the bedroom."

Mary knocked on the door at just after six and Persis, leaving Kerman sitting on the dressing-table stool and Maya, wearing the sari, carefully posed next to the window, went out, hissing over her shoulder, "Don't move, Maya, stay just as you are. You look perfect."

Returning a moment later, she threw the door wide, pulled Soshan forward and said, "There! Look at your beautiful Indian daughter. What do you think of her?"

There was a moment of total silence as Soshan stood motionless, her face pale, before bursting into tears. Maya froze and Persis was, for once, uncharacteristically speechless, her eyes wide with dismay.

At that moment John appeared in the doorway. "What is going on?" He went over to Maya and stood frowning down at her. She stared up at him helplessly, seemingly confined by her unfamiliar garment and unable to do or say anything.

Soshan sat down on the bed and made an ineffectual attempt to dry her eyes on her sleeve. "I'm sorry. Maya, you do look beautiful. Seeing you like this, something I never hoped for ...." Her voice cracked and she bent to hide her face.

Persis ran over and knelt beside her. "Soshan, don't. This is supposed to be a happy time for you." She took Soshan's hand and put her face against it. "For all of us. You know how glad we are to have you. How much we wanted to get to know Maya and share you with her. I didn't mean to upset you. Please don't cry." She too was in tears.

Kerman's eyes met John's. "I'm going to take Persis home." Her voice was level and firm. "We've done enough for one day. I'm not entirely sure what all this is about, Soshan, but for now we'll go and give you a chance to recover." For a second her voice quavered but she continued doggedly, "Maya wasn't too keen on the sari but don't be hard on my dear elder sister. She wanted to do something to please you." She pulled Persis to her feet, "Come on, we're seeing them all again tomorrow. Right now we have to go and leave them to themselves. Stop crying. No goodbyes. Just come!"

As Persis, with a forlorn backward look, went meekly with her, there was a fraught silence. Then Soshan said, "All this is my fault. It's just that I was shaken by seeing you as I have sometimes imagined you, Maya." She went over and lightly touched Maya's shoulder but sensing her withdrawal, stood hastily back and said vehemently, "Don't think for a moment that I want you to be anything other than what you have chosen to be." She paused but still getting no response, sighed and said sadly, "We both have to come to terms with how things are and do the best we can. Our immediate task is to get ready for this evening and, for your grandmother's sake, try to enjoy it. I'll just rinse my face and make it presentable and then go up to dress."

John waited until she had gone and then turned to Maya. He looked her up and down. "I don't understand what you are doing. You'd better take that off." He gestured at the sari, "It seems to have cast a spell on you. You haven't said a word all this time. You can see what a devastating effect it has had on your mother but that doesn't appear to have touched you at all. What on earth is the matter with you?"

"I don't know. I don't know. Don't look at me like that. I knew you would stop loving me if you saw what I'm like inside. I'm not furious with her anymore but I can't bear her crying over me. I can't take her tears. She hasn't any right to them." Maya banged her head against her clenched fists. "I knew this was a mistake. I shouldn't have given in to Persis but I could see how things have been for her and Kerman. This is such a milestone in their lives. I wanted to do something for them. This was the wrong thing to do." She looked up with a frown, distracted by a passing thought. "It really matters how you dress. People say it doesn't, that it's a superficial and unimportant thing, but clothes are symbolic. You dress to let people know how you see yourself." Her voice rose, "This isn't me and it's never going to be me. I should have held on to that. I am trying, John, but I still struggle to get things right."

"Calm down. Of course I haven't stopped loving you. But I will naturally get angry sometimes. You take everything too much to heart. Stop being a tragedy queen and remember that

I'm with you all the way." John took her in his arms. "Relax. You are doing well. By the way, you do look beautiful but while I'm not sure I agree about the symbolism of clothes, I see that this isn't something you take lightly. But you should. Just be yourself." He gave her a gentle smack on the bottom. "We'd better do as your mother said and get ready."

Soshan's two sisters and their husbands were sophisticated and extremely busy people. The men ran successful businesses and their wives not only provided them with comfortable, well managed homes but had active social lives of their own. All of them were much involved in the new and interesting careers on which their children, Maya's cousins, were currently embarking and these were the topics to which they continually returned. They had a strong, engrained sense of family duty and wanted to support Soshan, but though they made all the right gestures and asked carefully prepared, polite questions, they had no sustained interest in a niece who had ignored them all these years. A farmer and a primary school secretary did not have much to tell them. Maya did, though, make a conscious effort to convey one message, even if only by implication. It was also a message for her mother, an apology and a promise combined. Caught up in some lively conversation or other, she would call out and ask Soshan for confirmation of a point or ask her a question about something they had done together, giving a subtle impression of closeness and friendliness that, if it outran the actual, was a marker for the possible, and her mother's delighted response allowed them to put the earlier episode of the sari behind them. Generally the undemanding mood of the evening was a relief to Maya and probably was what

Soshan had expected even had she hoped for more from her sisters. In the end, they all parted satisfied with themselves, duty done.

Maya wanted to make her peace with Persis and played on her carefully designed rapport with Soshan a little shamelessly. "Could you take John off to one of your tourist places? I'll ask both the girls to come here for coffee. A morning with them putting right all that happened yesterday will be more worthwhile than seeing some monument or temple."

She was able to make this a fact by a frank admission to the sisters. "It must be incomprehensible to you but the question of what exactly I am, where I belong, has caused me such heart-burning that wearing a sari has a totally over-inflated significance for me. I'm glad you made me try, though, because it has helped me to get things straight in my mind. I can't do what you want, Persis. It really felt like wearing fancy dress to me and I don't want to spend time at the wedding thinking about myself and my appearance. I think about myself too much. I am ashamed when I see how brave you are and think of how self-pitying I can be. Your generosity to my mother sets me a shining example."

With everyone determinedly putting this incident behind them, Soshan, with some help from Persis and Kerman, virtuously took Maya and John round several noted tourist spots. Her unstated aim, though, was to give them an experience of what it was like to live here or even – a wilder ambition – to give them a sense of belonging, and they spent much of their time at lunches and dinners with relatives and friends or evenings at concerts and the cinema. After a few hectic days and before they had even begun to find their way around a bewilderment of strange customs and manners, exotic names and countless new faces, the day of the wedding was on them.

It was an understated affair. With the sad legacy of their previous marriages still casting a small shadow, Soshan and Sohrab wanted it that way. It took place at five in the evening in the Sethnas' drawing room and was a blandly official affair with two neighbours acting as witnesses and only the immediate family there. It was timed and planned as a mere prologue to the elaborate hotel reception that followed and, after a drink to the couple's health, everyone left to dress for that.

Here too, the bridal element was underplayed and having known these two as a couple for so long and partied in this way with them so often, their friends easily went along with this.

If the occasion meant more to their daughters, only a long, group hug and a few suppressed tears betrayed them as the three girls said goodbye to each other, not only at the end of the evening but the end of their time together. All the guests had gone and Soshan, exhausted by a long session of hand-shaking as they left, was sitting for moment in the hotel lobby with Sohrab while her parents went off to have a final word with the hotel manager.

"Come again soon, Maya. I think that if Kerman does make it to a university in England she will see you often and I will be very jealous unless you do." Persis, in college, and Kerman, in school, would not be seeing them off at the airport the next day.

They were booked on an early afternoon flight and Soshan and Sohrab, having rather reluctantly accepted this arrangement, had decided to leave at about the same time for their few days away together. Maya's grandparents, who had taken charge of them and would drive them to the airport, now came back to the lobby. There was no sign of the long day they had been through as, upright and undimmed, they chivvied everyone into action.

"Sohrab, take your family home. We'll see that these children are alright and get them off safely tomorrow. Soshan, you are very tired. Off you go now."

Soshan wordlessly held her arms out to Maya who, though still stiff and hesitant, allowed herself to be held and kissed, her face slightly averted. Then, what could now be seen as the Wadia family went off to Sohrab's flat, while she and John were led out to her grandparents' car.

If their immediate departure after the wedding day seemed eccentric, it saved them from any prolonged post mortems or sad farewells and Maya did have to get back for work. As their plane took off and she looked down on the receding city, she had to fight off an unexpected regret, but quickly recovered her nerve and was able to both look back at the last few days and forward to seeing her mother again in the summer with surprising calm.

"Everything has gone well. You have done well. I'm glad you decided to come. You are a good girl." John, leaning over to kiss her, was encouraged when she gave him a protesting smack on the hand at this patronising language and they spent the rest of the flight in good humour with each other and a pleasurable anticipation of soon being home.

TWENTY-ONE

"It's like science fiction," Maya said, as landing at Heathrow, they reset their watches to local time. "Seven o'clock. We're going back in time. We're going to live the past four and a half hours all over again. I feel a bit exhausted at the mere idea."

"I'm just exhausted. I don't need any ideas to do that to me. But come on, we'll be home in time for a hot bath, a hot drink and a long sleep." John trundled their luggage out of the building. "Doesn't the thought of needing something hot strike you as a very good idea?" He breathed in the cool damp of a cloudy April evening with deep satisfaction.

They reached the farm just as Robert, Joyce and Mrs Fielding had abandoned any thought of waiting up for them and gone upstairs. They did come down again in dressing gowns to say hello but were happy to defer any travelogues until the morning. It was all very relaxed and unexcitable after the high voltage behaviours they had left behind.

Since Robert and John were out around the farm early as always, and breakfast was a series of staggered sittings, it was not until eleven that they all managed to gather for coffee and a chance to look at photographs and discuss the trip and the wedding. Joyce was already packed and ready to go home immediately after this and John was planning the return trip for Maya's grandmother. Later, however, there was a call from Peter.

"John, how was India? Noisy, dirty and exasperating, I'm sure. How was the wedding?" Without waiting for an answer, he continued, "Look, I don't want you to have to chauffeur Mother. I will come and fetch her. If it is convenient, maybe I could come tomorrow, stay overnight and take her home the following day."

When John told them all that he had agreed to this plan, Robert was neutral, Mrs. Fielding surprised and delighted and Maya annoyed.

"Dad's worming his way into our life. I don't want him here." Avoiding any confrontation with John but needing to voice her discontent, she spoke peevishly to her grandmother, then seeing her face fall, said contritely, "I'm sorry. It's good that he is coming to fetch you and I shouldn't be ungracious. But he is a bit demanding about when and how he does that, you must admit."

"He liked it here when he came last time. He got on well with Robert and John and is interested in their rental business. He enjoys having a chance to give advice. As for fetching me, I realise that he's probably merely asserting his right to control my affairs," she smiled thinly, "but it's encouraging to think he even wants to do that. Be patient with him, Maya. He can't harm you anymore and having him here will please John. It could be worse. At least he isn't imposing Karen on you. I don't want to be unkind, but he probably sees this as a temporary escape from her."

Whatever his reasons for coming, Peter behaved well. He made a valiant effort to show an interest in their holiday, asked polite questions about the wedding, took time to look at the photographs, and made a point of deferring to Maya over the timing of meals and how best to fit in with their household arrangements. Robert assumed over-all charge of him and at supper the three men were so engrossed in their own topics of conversation that Maya took her grandmother into her room for the evening and shut the door on them. Secretly, she found having her father here under the civilising influence of John's family, tacitly acknowledging that she was the mistress of the house, rather gratifying.

Back at work, she shared her photographs and impressions of her holiday with her colleagues, ending the slight constraint that still hovered between them on the subject of her Indian connection. Experiences of heat and dust and noisy neighbours were, though, already a fading memory when, two weeks after their return, India burst in on her again in the form of a letter from Persis.

Bombay
20/4/15

My dearest Maya,

We are missing you so much already and I have something important to tell you. But first I am going to be serious and swear you to secrecy when I admit that we found the wedding, a big thing for us, a little disappointing and unromantic. I do understand why it was that way. In fact, and this is another total secret, although we love your mother dearly and wanted her to marry Dad, it has been a little harder than we expected to see her always here with him in the flat, doing the things that our mother used to do. But our dearest father understands us so well and, in cahoots with your Sethna grandparents, has come up with a plan. Kerman and I are going to move into Soshan's flat. What do you think of that? We are made to understand that there will be strict surveillance 'from above'. Your grandmother has given us a stern talking-to. There will be no wild parties or unladylike behaviour! This move also solves the problem of what to do with Mary. Soshan was very worried about how she would deal with this big change and what sort of meaningful work we could find for her. Now she will chaperone us and can stay in her familiar rooms and still enjoy her gossips with the servants upstairs. She is already full of herself at the thought of having two younger versions of Soshan to look after and to bully a little. We shall also be given the partial use of Swami and the car as your mother will share Dad's car and driver. I will write again soon but I wanted to send this news which we find very exciting. Do write to me often. Let's write. I don't want these thoughts stamped on the ether! Give my fondest love to John and tell him I am looking already for a man just like him though I don't hope for one with his gorgeous blue eyes!!

Your affectionate semi-sister

Persis.

Attached to this was a hand-drawn cartoon showing a large figure, recognisably Mary, wagging a finger at two smaller figures, sitting in front of her with bowed heads. Maya could not stop smiling, but while she wanted an end to the sadness, so poignant if so underplayed in this bright letter, she felt a sneaking relief that Kerman and Persis would not be living with Soshan. It was mean-minded and ungenerous but it had upset her to think of them in such intimate, daily contact with her mother. The letter also reminded her of her grandmother's earlier judgement on her ex-daughter-in-law. "Your mother was very young and had led a very privileged life. She was full of romantic ideas and reality was a bit of a shock for her." Here was a vivid evocation of just how privileged life could be for such girls. Even if the home that Peter provided had been relatively comfortable, the reality that had confronted her would hardly have measured up and must have come as a considerable shock to the twenty-one year old Soshan. Maya might at one level view Persis and Kerman with childish jealousy but her sympathy for them had opened her to new ways of seeing things. Through them she had entered more fully into her mother's world and found herself, for the first time, able to empathise with her feelings as an individual, a personality with a separate story of her own.

She was sitting in the garden gateway, the letter in her hand. It was a chilly morning and her recent and short experience of heat having apparently thinned her blood and made her more susceptible to the cold, she was wrapped up in a thick jacket but, looking towards the trees, she saw a hint of green, like a watercolour wash across a charcoal sketch that hinted at coming warmth and lushness. This was such a familiar, peaceful view but today she was seeing it with enhanced appreciation, making comparisons with the very different scenes that had so recently assailed her senses. She did not miss those. She certainly did not miss the endless noise that, on her return, had made the silence here almost painful, as if a pressure on her ears had been too quickly removed. Yet India, so long and so determinedly resisted, had insidiously stamped itself on her mind and was threatening to invade her heart, if only because it was the country that shaped and made sense of these new people who had already done just that.

To put India in its place and tie herself firmly back to Home Farm, she now got John started on the delayed re-decoration of their bedroom and went shopping for additions to her own room. She managed to find a companion piece to complement Robert's painting that almost matched her imagined interior and she bought two pretty rugs and some houseplants. This private space had become an important symbol of her increasing self-confidence. As she finished arranging her acquisitions, she stood in the centre of it and turned round slowly. "Maya's room," she thought with immense pleasure. She looked back over a slow process of change – the experiences of loss and death, the growing awareness of, and willingness to accommodate, the needs and urges that drove other people, her gradual acceptance by John's family and the fortunate chance that had brought her to this perfect place – a process that, like a developing bud bursting into flower, had produced a dramatic and apparently instantaneous change, all the old questions of who she was, where she belonged, answered. She danced childishly round the room. "I am what I am. I'm where I belong. I'm John's wife. I'm safe at last."

This new certainty and optimism made the increasingly frequent visits of her father, who was entering into John's renovations of the farm buildings with enthusiasm, unexpectedly tolerable. Indeed, seeing them one morning, standing outside one of the almost completed cottages, their heads together over a fluttering plan that John was trying to hold steady in the wind, she was surprised at the affectionate glow she felt. She was even able to welcome Karen on the one occasion when she came for the day, achieving an easy rapport with her by talking about fashion and describing the fabrics and leather goods that Persis had shown her.

She had also embarked on another personal project, taking on the upkeep of the kitchen garden and supervising the renovation of the hen runs there, intending to increase the number of poultry they kept and consider going on at some stage to something commercially viable. Joyce was her willing helper and mentor and they spent hours there together, digging and planting and chatting.

"It's going to transform my memories of this place, working in it with you." Joyce smiled at Maya as she struggled up from kneeling beside one of the raised beds. "I'm rather more creaky but definitely happier than when I gardened here as a girl."

"I'm happier than I've ever been." Maya also stood up, looking down on the neat rows of plants they had put in. "I'm storing new memories. It's good to know that I shall never need to regret or alter anything when I revisit these."

The weeks were passing so pleasantly and so quickly that it took a letter from her mother giving definite dates for her visit to Europe with Sohrab to shock Maya out of an unthinking euphoria and make her realise how soon the summer holiday would be upon her. With no possible excuse for delay or denial, she had to dispel any lingering doubts and ask them both to stay, if only for an experimental weekend.

"Maya, I've had a great idea." John sounded unusually excited. "I know you still worry about Soshan and Sohrab staying here. Why don't we put them in one of the cottages? We can explain that, like Soshan giving us her flat, we're doing it to give them privacy and space. It would be a useful trial. I can ask them to tell me frankly how it is for guests."

"You sound like my father. No, sorry, don't look like that." Maya ran to him and gave him a warm kiss. "You know that when it comes to anything to do with my parents, I revert to my petty, nasty, little self. It's a very good idea. It will also make things bearable for Robert. He's let me take charge in the house but I know that he has moments when he misses the way things used to be. I don't think he looks forward to accommodating strangers."

Robert had spoken to Joyce about this in a way that confirmed this view of his state of mind and led Joyce, as usual, to reprimand and lecture him.

"That bothers me a bit, all these plans for Maya's mother and her husband to stay with us. I don't know that I want to see the house full of Indians."

"Robert! You can't say things like that. For goodness sake don't let Maya know what you are thinking. And never say it to anyone else. It's not a good idea these days."

"I know all about keeping things that can't be said to myself." Robert looked straight at his sister, as close as he had ever been to voicing a shared, unspoken knowledge. "The trouble is that what you can and can't say keeps changing. It's hard to keep up. But I won't risk hurting Maya. She's a good girl. It is odd though. When I sometimes come on her, catch sight of her unexpectedly, what I see is a small foreigner. That's a bit of a shock. Then, when I look again, I see Maya."

"Yes, well we are both learning a lot from having her in the family. I'm sure it has done us good and that having her mother and her new husband here will do the same. Mind you, I think we can also say that being with us has done Maya good too. It's not all one-way traffic. It's been good for all of us."

Maya, having checked that Robert had no worries about her visitors that using the cottage could not overcome, also made sure that Mrs Hemsby was ready to cater to them without any qualms. Sharing with her plans for a lunch party during their stay that couldn't be put on without her expert help appeared to override any that she might have had.

With John persuasive and enthusiastic, Soshan and Sohrab were asked to stay for a full week. They would arrive on the fourth of August. Peter and Karen accepted an invitation to lunch on the Saturday of that week and would bring his mother. Mariam had to refuse their invitation as she would be on holiday with a friend. So it was to be a family affair, a tight little gathering together of her extended family. A wave of panic, the stuff of her earlier nightmares, washed over Maya, leaving her weak and shaky. The gulf between decision and deed yawned. She walked around her garden, sat gazing out over the now green and inviting view beyond its gate, went indoors to spend several calming moments in her room, all to hold onto her resolve, but as the time drew closer, this continued to waver and had she dared she might have opted out of the whole thing.

TWENTY- TWO

For the first two days of August, the weather matched Maya's unexpected and unhelpful descent into gloomy anxiety. The sun disappeared completely behind heavy, dark clouds and, though it stayed dry, there was a constant threat of showers. On the morning of Soshan and Sohrab's arrival, though, there was a break in those clouds and by the time they drove up to the door in a hired car, just before midday, the early, rather fitful sunshine had settled into something more promising.

Standing in the porch, Maya looked round at John, Robert and Joyce who had followed her out. "Well," she thought with a dark, sustaining humour, "I may have invited the enemy inside the gates but I now have a praetorian guard to keep me safe and protect my happiness." She reached out for John's hand. He looked down at her and gave hers an encouraging squeeze. Recalling her desperate voice, such a short time ago – "I don't want her here. I don't want her anywhere near here." – he was overcome by a huge relief as he realised how far they had come from that disheartening point.

"Maya," Sohrab, first out of the car, came over and kissed her cheek, "I have letters and gifts from Persis and Kerman. They're quite upset that we have come without them." He shook hands with John who introduced him to the others. Soshan, emerging more slowly, put her hand very lightly on Maya's cheek. "Darling, you look so well." She hugged John. "It's good to see you again," – releasing him, she turned to Robert and Joyce – "and to have a chance to meet your family."

John explained where they would be staying and, the introductions over, took them straight to the cottage and saw that they were comfortably installed there before returning to the farmhouse with them for lunch.

"Maya has told us a lot about the farm but nothing had prepared us for just how charming it is. How lucky you are to have lived here all your life." Soshan dazzled Robert with her smile. He was as charmed by her as she was by the farm. She had come dressed in dark cords, a white blouse and sensible shoes and was as far from his image of an Indian woman as it was possible to be. Joyce, guarded and cautious around someone who had hurt Maya so badly and, if she were honest, whose elegance rather intimidated her, was more taken by Sohrab. His manners reminded her of an old-fashioned and much regretted past and his quiet, good sense appealed to all that was down-to-earth in her own nature.

Soshan was struggling to suppress her jealousy of this surrogate mother, living so close to her daughter and seeing her almost daily. She caught every nuance of the easy camaraderie that existed between Maya and Joyce, registering the number of times that they spoke of shared interests and joint tasks. She might remind herself that this was a just reward for her past sins and that she had to be thankful for any sharing she was allowed, but theory is one thing. In practice, it was hard to take.

John, realising what a momentous advance this visit was, what trauma and inhibitions Maya had overcome, what reservations Robert and to a lesser extent Joyce might have about these foreign guests, had anticipated some strain, even friction, however politely disguised, and to counteract this had arranged a busy programme that kept Soshan and Sohrab fully occupied. He and Maya took them for a full day out in Norwich that ended with an evening at the theatre, followed this with another full day in Cambridge, then a day exploring the seaside towns along the North Norfolk coast. While Maya excused herself, pleading the work that needed to be done for the coming party as a reason for staying at home after all this, he took them on a couple of tours of the local area, showing them some of the county's lovely old churches and treating them to lunch at two of its more picturesque pubs.

These excursions provided a range of uncontroversial and general topics for conversation as they all gathered for supper each evening and by the end of the week these had become extremely agreeable occasions. Sohrab and John had built on an earlier rapport arising from common interests and temperamental affinity and always had a great deal to say to each other and Joyce, drawn to Sohrab by a similar likeness, had become totally relaxed with him. Robert was more and more taken with Soshan, her chic appearance and sophisticated manner appealing to the latent dandy in him. Maya and her mother, initially careful with each other, were caught up in this general atmosphere of conviviality and less and less constrained as the days passed. Maya even took Soshan into her room and showed her all the things she had so carefully arranged there but closed the door on it firmly after this inspection, leaving it unused for the rest of the week. It was still a concession too far to sit there with her.

On the morning of the lunch party, though, they were both up early and checking over the arrangements together. Soshan went into the kitchen and spoke to Mrs Hemsby with the easy authority of someone who had lived with servants all her life. "You have worked miracles. It would take four people at home in India to do what you have done. I've told Maya what a treasure you are." Her praise made Mrs Hemsby's cheeks glow with pride. Asking herself why she was so comfortable with what she should have seen as irritating interference, Maya recognised their common urge to put on a good show for Peter. The past was still powerful and for the first time in that long saga of hurts and humiliations she and her mother were on the same side.

When Peter did arrive, he did so with far less fanfare than usual and came quietly and slowly into the hall with his mother holding on to his arm and Karen, for whom this was less familiar territory, following them carrying two gift bags. Joyce emerged from the dining room to greet them. "Well, it's not much of a welcome on such an occasion is it? John and Robert have gone off to see what's happening in one of the fields and Maya and Soshan are doing something last minute in the kitchen. Go and make yourselves comfortable in the sitting room and I'll tell them that you are here."

Peter raised his eyes at the thought of Maya and Soshan in domestic harmony but having settled his mother and Karen, went off to find John and Robert. Suddenly, as if to make up for this lack of a ceremonial welcome, everyone crowded into the sitting room at once. Maya and Soshan came in with Joyce just as Sohrab, who had stayed in the cottage for a little time alone, also arrived. Peter, following closely, gave him a cool nod and, rather flamboyantly, kissed first Maya and then Soshan, who gave him a quizzical look. John and Robert, showing signs of a quick wash, also hurried in, apologised for not having been on hand earlier and began to take orders for drinks.

Half an hour later Mrs Hemsby called them in to lunch and by the time that she and Maya finally cleared the table and brought in coffee nearly two hours after that, delicious food, wine and animated conversation had produced a pervasive mood of friendliness and informality. As she went round the table, Maya stood for a moment behind John, catching the familiar citrus note of his aftershave and resisting a strong temptation to kiss the back of his neck. He turned to look up at her and a silent message passed between them in a language now well understood by them both. She moved on and he turned back to Sohrab, the two of them lingering over their cooling coffee as they became engrossed in serious discussion.

Peter, foregoing this male bonding for once, turned to Karen. "I'd like to show you the last cottage that John has been working on. You must spread the word about them among your friends and if you've seen one it will help you to enthuse them." He took her out through the hall and the front door, offering his arm as she struggled with her fashionable shoes. Joyce and Mrs Fielding retired to the sitting room and more comfortable chairs for a quiet chat and were joined by Robert who soon lost the thread of what they were saying and dozed off, snoring gently.

Maya and Soshan both in need of fresh air after a long morning and far too much food, went and stood by the back door.

"Is this the garden that I've heard you and Joyce talking about?" Soshan who had not been out here before could not help wondering if this had been more than mere chance, if she had been deliberately excluded all this time. There was a note in her voice that made Maya look at her closely. "Are you upset by that?" she asked bluntly.

"Yes, if I'm honest. No," her voice rose and she said explosively, "I'm not merely upset. I'm racked with regret. Seeing you with Joyce is very painful. This has been a good week but it has brought home to me just what I threw away when I went off and left you. It is entirely my fault but it doesn't help to know that. We are getting by. We are coming closer and I hope that from now on we will share the important things in our lives, but nothing can give us back that lost time."

"Don't be jealous of Joyce. Don't be misled by her placid exterior. In her own way, she too regrets a lost daughter. She suffered a late miscarriage before she had John. I'm a substitute for a girl who was never born. And she lost a husband. That was very hard because they were close and they really loved each other." She looked squarely, pointedly, at Soshan. "Come over here. I'll show you my favourite view, the place where Joyce got engaged."

They went over to the gateway and Maya sat down. Soshan, looking dubiously at the ground and then at her smart trousers, slowly sat down beside her.

"You and John have both lectured me about how to remember the past. Well, ever since I first saw it, this has been a place where I have come to think things over." Maya glanced at Soshan and said thoughtfully, "This is Joyce's past to me. When she was young, walking with a quiet man whom she loved, in a quiet, country meadow, she expected to be quietly happy ever after. Anyone would have expected her to be. But tragedy isn't restricted to the extreme and the exotic and it didn't work out that way." Again Maya looked squarely at Soshan. "We imagine that we are a special case; that we live special, unusual lives. We felt entitled to dwell endlessly on what went wrong for us. Joyce never does that. She just bravely gets on with things. We need to be more like her. Let's call a truce and think only of the future. I said that I see this as Joyce's past. I sit here. She doesn't. And I have never done more than sit and contemplate it. But this isn't a memento, a postcard or a painting. I've watched it go from summer greenery to bare bleakness and back again. It's a living place that changes with the seasons. A message for us don't you think? In a while, I'm going to fetch Joyce and the three of us will actually walk there together."

John's conversation with Sohrab petered out a little and he got up and looked round for Maya. He wanted to see her slight figure as he had last seen her, her face a little flushed with her exertions and her rather wild hair, as always, escaping the band she had fixed it with. He wanted to see her and be reassured that she was alright. He wanted to see her.

He could not find her anywhere in the house and went to look outside. He stood in the back doorway and his face lightened. Two slim figures were sitting in the far gateway, dark heads close. One of them had her arm around the other's waist. He did not want anything to interrupt that silent, peaceful communication. With a sigh of immense satisfaction, he went inside and closed the door.

Other Books by Joan Khurody

No-One Mentioned Bandits

Into the Night with a Stranger

Available from – YPD Books and Amazon

and

Joan Khurody

see links on www.joankhurody.co.uk